"I'll Braid Your Hair if You'd Like."

Hawk gathered her hair into both his hands, smoothing it, stroking the glossy waves.

She refused to look at him, still unused to her reaction to his touch. She nodded and stood quietly as he began to plait her hair into one long braid, tying it off at last and letting it fall to her waist.

"You have beautiful hair," he said gruffly, stepping back from her. She turned around to thank him, the words dying on her lips when she saw the look in his eyes. They were blazing with intense heat, and his look scorched her with its message of desire.

"Hawk..."

She didn't know what she intended to say, but he gave her no chance before his arms came around her.

Dear Reader,

Welcome to Silhouette! Our goal is to give you hours of unbeatable reading pleasure, and we hope you'll enjoy each month's six new Silhouette Desires. These sensual, provocative love stories are both believable and compelling—sometimes they're poignant, sometimes humorous, but always enjoyable.

Indulge yourself. Experience all the passion and excitement of falling in love along with our heroine as she meets the irresistible man of her dreams and together they overcome all obstacles in the path to a happy ending.

If this is your first Desire, I hope it'll be the first of many. If you're already a Silhouette Desire reader, thanks for your support! Look for some of your favorite authors in the coming months: Stephanie James, Diana Palmer, Dixie Browning, Ann Major and Doreen Owens Malek, to name just a few.

Happy reading!

Isabel Swift
Senior Editor

SDRL-7/85

ANNETTE BROADRICK
Hawk's Flight

Silhouette Desire

Published by Silhouette Books New York

America's Publisher of Contemporary Romance

SILHOUETTE BOOKS
300 E. 42nd St., New York, N.Y. 10017

Copyright © 1985 by Annette Broadrick

Distributed by Pocket Books

ISBN: 0-373-05242-1

First Silhouette Books printing November 1985

10 9 8 7 6 5 4 3 2 1

America's Publisher of Contemporary Romance

Printed in the U.S.A.

Books by Annette Broadrick

Silhouette Romance

Circumstantial Evidence #329
Provocative Peril #359

Silhouette Desire

Hunter's Prey #185
Bachelor Father #219
Hawk's Flight #242

ANNETTE BROADRICK

has been a reader of romantic fiction for a number of years and has discovered a special joy in being able to write what she most enjoys reading. She gets totally involved with her characters, which perhaps explains why her readers do, too.

This one is for you, Michelle—for your loving support when I needed it the most—with my love.

One

———

Hawk waited.

When virtues were handed out, Hawk somehow missed out on patience. He didn't handle waiting around well, and today was no exception. He glanced at his watch.

What's keeping Dr. Winston? His office called almost an hour ago to charter a plane.

Hawk stood in the cramped office of Horizon Aviation Service, his elbow resting on the counter. The doctor, whom he'd never met, needed to fly to Flagstaff due to some family emergency. Hawk had been the only one available to take the flight, causing him to postpone his vacation plans for a few hours.

Oh, well. It wouldn't be the first time he'd had to change his plans. Come to think of it, when had any of his plans *ever* worked out as he expected?

Not that he'd minded helping his friend Rick get the
charter service going in El Paso, but it had brought
him back to the States a year earlier than he'd intended. Now that Horizon Aviation was solidly established Hawk knew it was time for him to be making
new plans.

He never stayed in one place too long. A restless
nature and an inquisitive mind kept him on the move.

Hawk was ready for change—he definitely needed
the vacation. Eighteen months of long hours and hard
work had taken their toll. He pictured himself hiking
into the mountains of Mexico's interior, enjoying the
solitude and the tranquility of nature.

*If the good doctor will get a move on, we'll be in
Flagstaff in a few hours. With a good night's sleep, I
can be flying south by sunup tomorrow.*

Hawk caught a glimpse of a late-model car through
the office door and he watched as it pulled in across
the street. A young woman threw open the driver's
door and leaped out, ignoring the wavering heat waves
that rose from the sizzling asphalt of the airport's
parking lot. Her rose-colored summer suit, although
flattering to her petite figure, made her look over-
dressed for the hot Texas sun.

She hurried to the back of her car and opened the
trunk lid. When she leaned over, Hawk admired the
way her slim skirt clung to her curves. It also revealed
a pair of very shapely legs. He slowly straightened
from his leaning position at the counter. She was a
good-looking woman, no doubt about it.

Grabbing a small bag out of the trunk, she slammed
the lid and started across the pavement toward him,
her high heels sinking slightly in the heat-softened
surface. Hawk had to revise his original opinion of her

as she came closer. The woman was more than good-looking—she was stunning!

He tried to understand his strong reaction to her. Maybe it was because she wore a look of fragility—she was small with delicate features. Maybe it was her fair complexion that gave her a porcelain-doll appearance. With her soft ivory coloring she was either a visitor to the dry desert air of El Paso or she spent all of her time indoors.

He caught a flash of fiery red in her dark brown hair where the sun picked out highlights. She wore it in a jaunty topknot, with wispy curls framing her face. Hawk wondered about the color of her eyes, hidden by sunglasses.

Her skin glowed and he could almost feel its silkiness as though he'd already experienced the sensation of running his hand along her cheek. His palm tingled.

What's happening to me? he wondered. He'd seen beautiful women before, and she wasn't even his type. Women who looked like she did were notoriously spoiled, and that was a breed he was careful to avoid. *The heat must be getting to me.*

He wondered what she was doing there. He glanced at Rick, who was taking flight charter information over the phone. *Maybe he's got himself a new girl and didn't want me to know. I'll have to tease him about being afraid I'd try to cut in on his territory.*

They both knew that would never happen. Hawk had a standard attitude toward women—he could take 'em or leave 'em. He generally left them—before they decided to discuss a more permanent arrangement.

His gaze returned to the woman rapidly approaching the door. She was different from the women he'd known in a way he couldn't define, and it made him uneasy. He could feel a tightening deep within him, as though warning him to prepare to do battle with his reactions to her.

Hawk deliberately straightened and turned away from the door. He leaned both elbows on the counter. *That's enough ogling for one day,* he reminded himself. *I wish to hell the good doctor would get here if he's got such an all-fired emergency!*

Paige swung open the heavy glass door to the air charter service and stepped inside the refreshingly cool room, pausing to remove her sunglasses and to adjust her eyes after the white glare of the July sun. She looked around the tiny office, wondering if she'd made the right decision. When her receptionist managed to charter a plane for her, she was so grateful she hadn't questioned her further.

Paige glanced around the room with dismay, beginning to have second thoughts. Large maps, posters and calendars cluttered the walls. A battered desk and two nondescript chairs waited for occupants on the public side of the counter, while another desk and miscellaneous office equipment sat in a crowded jumble behind it.

Two men occupied the office. One was standing in front of the waist-high counter, and the other was talking on the phone in the office section.

She wondered how long the man at the counter had been waiting. She glanced at her watch, then determinedly walked over to the counter, hoping the man on the phone would glance up. She needed to be on her way—now.

"Were you looking for someone?"

Paige stared up at the man beside her. Seen up close, he looked almost intimidating. He appeared to be at least six feet tall, but it was his build she found most disquieting.

He was broad-shouldered, with muscled arms emphasized by the khaki shirt he wore, the sleeves rolled up halfway between his shoulder and elbow. Thick, black hair fell across his forehead, and his face had the high cheekbones and rich skin tones that generally denoted some Indian blood, which wasn't an unusual sight in the southwest. His voice had a full-bodied, rich sound that created a slight tingling within her. She forced herself to meet his black eyes. The man looked tough as well as formidable. Whatever he was thinking, he gave nothing away.

Paige decided she didn't have time to waste, and perhaps he could help her. "Actually, I'm here to charter a plane," she explained.

He stiffened, staring at her with suspicion. "Your name is—"

"Paige Winston."

"*Doctor* Winston?" A note of disbelief crept into his voice.

"That's right." She glanced at the man on the phone, who had yet to acknowledge her presence. "Do you know how much longer he'll be?"

The man shrugged. "It doesn't matter—I'm your pilot. I'm ready to go whenever you are."

"*You're* my pilot?" she asked in surprise.

"Yes. I understand you need to get to Flagstaff right away."

The slight doubt in his tone brought her to her senses. She didn't care who was flying her, so long as she got there as soon as possible. "Yes. Yes, I do. My father's been vacationing near Flagstaff and had a heart attack." She brushed her fingers distractedly through the curls that clung to her forehead. "He's in the hospital there now."

He nodded, then reached over and picked up the small bag resting at her feet. Motioning her to a door she hadn't noticed, he said, "This way."

The blinding sun hit Paige like a furnace blast of heat and glare and she quickly fumbled for her sunglasses. When she got them on she discovered the pilot was halfway to a small plane sitting on the edge of the runway.

Her heart pounded in her chest. She was expected to fly in *that*? It was so small! She glanced around nervously, but saw nothing bigger. The pilot turned around and stared at her, frowning slightly. He, too, had placed sunglasses over his eyes, but his were mirrored and Paige saw only her own reflection as she hurried up to him, breathless from the heat and her fear of the small plane.

He held out his hand, and when Paige placed hers uncertainly into it, he lifted her to the wing of the plane, motioning for her to crawl into the tiny door that was before her.

Paige discovered her suit was not the most practical choice of apparel for the trip, but then, she hadn't given it a thought when she'd rushed home and thrown a few things in a bag. All she could think about was her father.

How serious was his heart attack? What condition would he be in when she arrived? He had to be all right. He *had* to be. Not only was he her parent, but he was her business partner and best friend as well. She couldn't survive without him!

Paige scrambled inside, tugging at her skirt as she slid into the seat next to the pilot's position. She glanced around, bewildered at the gauges and switches that covered the dash. A small steering mechanism was in front of her, and she fervently prayed she wasn't expected to know anything about it.

Hawk followed her into the plane, made sure her seat belt was properly fastened, then settled into the seat next to her, checking that he had all the necessary maps and papers for the flight. He'd already gone through the preflight checklist before she arrived, knowing that saving time was important, but he ran an experienced glance over everything one more time.

He picked up the mike and contacted the control tower, requesting takeoff instructions. Within minutes they were airborne.

Paige watched the brown baked surface of El Paso fall away below their plane as they climbed. Mount Franklin continued to perform its centuries-old sentinel duty overlooking the sprawling city.

"You okay?"

Paige gave a nervous jerk when the pilot spoke. What was there about the man that caused her to overreact to him? He was polite enough, so that wasn't it. It had something to do with the sound of his voice—as though somehow she should recognize it. Yet she knew she'd never seen him before in her life.

Paige glanced at him and nodded. "I'm fine." She cleared her throat. "When do you expect to reach Flagstaff?"

He studied the instruments in front of him for a moment, a slight frown creasing his brow. Then he smiled at her. His teeth flashed white against his bronzed complexion. "We're due in by seven, barring complications."

"What sort of complications?" she asked nervously.

"There's a storm moving in from the north that I'm hoping to avoid. That may mean flying due west, then north. It could mean a longer flight, but it will be a much more comfortable ride."

She shuddered. She'd never cared for flying, even in large commercial planes. This small one made her feel she was barely balanced in the air.

Trying to sound calm, Paige said, "I'm so glad I was able to charter a plane on such short notice." She knew she was chattering, but she needed to get her mind off her thoughts.

"An hour later and you'd been out of luck."

"You mean you'd have been gone on another charter?"

The corner of his mouth turned up in a slight smile. "No, ma'am. I'd have been gone on my vacation."

"Oh!" Paige wondered if he'd been upset about having to take her. She couldn't tell. "I'm sorry," she offered.

"No problem. I intend to spend the night in Flagstaff and leave for Mexico in the morning."

"Do you have family in Mexico?"

"No. A friend of mine has a large hacienda down in the interior. It's got a landing strip I intend to use. I plan to backpack into the mountains and do some fishing."

"By yourself?"

He looked at her in surprise. "Sure."

She couldn't imagine spending a vacation alone. For that matter, she couldn't imagine spending a vacation camping. The Great Outdoors was a total mystery to her and she'd never had any desire to get better acquainted.

"I'm glad I didn't ruin your plans for you."

"Don't worry. You didn't."

"Have you been flying long?" she heard herself blurt out. She hadn't meant to sound so apprehensive, but it was too late to rephrase her question.

He grinned again and her heart tripled its already rapid beat. He had a beautiful smile, one that stirred up all sorts of butterflies within her that had nothing to do with her nervousness.

"About twenty years."

"Twenty!" She stared at him in disbelief. He couldn't be much older than her thirty years.

"I've been flying since I was sixteen."

"Wasn't that a little young to start?"

"I suppose, but I'd been on my own since I was fourteen. I made friends with a pilot and was underfoot so much of the time he finally hired me to work around his aviation service. I think he finally started teaching me how to fly to stop all my pestering questions."

His comments created all sorts of questions in her mind. Where was his family during that time? Why had he left home? It occurred to her that she didn't even know his name.

"I'm afraid you have me at a disadvantage. You know my name but I don't know yours."

"Hawk."

"Hawk?"

"That's right."

She wondered if that were a nickname but didn't want to press. Instead she stared out the window, trying not to think about how far off the ground they were.

"What made you decide to become a doctor?"

His deep voice interrupted her nervous thoughts, although his question didn't particularly surprise her. She'd spent most of her life answering that question in one form or another.

"Several reasons, actually," she admitted. "My father is a doctor—a pediatrician. I can't remember a time when I didn't want to be a doctor as well. And I love children. I've never been sorry for following in my father's footsteps. We have a clinic in El Paso."

"How long have you been a doctor?"

"Four years."

"You must have started rather young yourself. You barely look old enough to vote," he stated with a slow smile.

"I've been old enough to vote for several years now."

He smiled at her prim tone, then picked up the mike and spoke into it. When a disembodied voice responded, he asked for an update of the storm moving in, then listened intently as the voice rattled off what to Paige was incomprehensible data about clouds, winds and air currents.

She knew there was no reason for her to worry about the weather. He was obviously staying on top of things. She just wished she could get her queasy stomach to understand that, not to mention her racing pulse.

"Have you flown much?" His question was a welcome diversion.

"Uh, no, I haven't."

His smile was very reassuring. "Why don't you just relax, lay your head back and close your eyes. You'd be surprised how that helps."

Paige nodded, knowing it would be ridiculous to deny her nervousness. A perfectly good tissue lay shredded in her lap. He probably wouldn't believe an explanation that shredding tissues was a new hobby of hers.

She closed her eyes with a quiet determination, but her father immediately came to mind and they flashed open once more. *Your worrying won't contribute to his recovery,* she reminded herself.

Paige glanced over at Hawk, covertly studying his profile. She found him intriguing—he was different from anyone she'd ever met. He seemed to have forgotten her as he donned earphones. She could no longer hear the radio.

Slowly and imperceptibly, Paige began to relax. The work load at the clinic had been heavy since her father had been gone and she knew she'd been overdoing it. *Oh, Dad, please be all right.* Her loving message winged its way to him. She hoped he knew of her concern. *I'll be with you in a few short hours. Please hang on.*

Her long lashes dropped one last time, then stayed down. Paige slept.

It was some time later when Hawk spared a glance in her direction. She really must have been tired to be sleeping through the increasingly rough gusts of wind that grabbed the plane and shook it—like a giant hand wanting to play.

He didn't care for the approaching storm or the way the oil pressure gauge was acting. He'd spent the entire morning working on that oil line and had been convinced he'd discovered and repaired the problem. *So what the hell's wrong with the gauge?*

Paige was jolted awake by a thundering crash. She glanced out the window of the plane and recoiled in horror. Black rolling clouds seemed to engulf them. She looked at Hawk and noted his grim expression as he wrestled the plane through the swirling wind currents.

"It looks like the storm you mentioned earlier found us," she said, trying to mask her concern.

Without looking at her, he nodded. "Right now the storm is the least of our worries."

"What do you mean?"

"I've got to put this baby down in the first available space. We're losing oil pressure."

She looked down, but could see nothing but angry dark clouds. What had happened to the sunlight?

"Where are we?"

"Eastern Arizona," he said in a terse tone.

She tried to remember her geography. What was in eastern Arizona? Hopefully it was desert and saguaro cactus. Or was that the Phoenix area?

Hawk continued to bring the plane down to a lower elevation, praying to break free of the clouds shortly, giving him some visual idea of where they could land.

His prayer was answered almost immediately. The dark clouds began to thin out and patches of green appeared. So far, so good. He glanced back at the oil pressure gauge. It was still dropping.

Paige saw the land and felt her heart leap in her chest. Mountains. Green-covered mountains. Would he find a place flat enough to land?

Once again she stared at the man who held their lives in his hands. He'd removed his glasses, and, except for the slight frown line between his brows, his expression was impassive. She wondered if Indians were taught that look or whether it came to them naturally. She was certain her fear was written in large block letters across her face.

It was too late to ask herself if she trusted the man. Much too late. After all, it was his life as much as it was hers. But she knew nothing about his skills or his background, and she recognized how foolish she'd been not to find out more about him before taking off in the plane.

But would it have made any difference? Her receptionist had tried to find other ways to get to Flagstaff. Chartering the plane had been the quickest, at least it had seemed so at the time.

Paige glanced down again, then wished she hadn't. The ground was coming up closer at an alarming rate. She took a quick breath of relief when Hawk leveled off, skimming the tops of the large ponderosa pine trees that dotted the land. Paige could see no place where he could safely land the plane.

Hawk shared her thought but refused to panic. He'd been in tight spots before. He forced himself to remember landings he'd made in southeast Asia, in Central and South America, when he'd been able to put his plane down in very little space. But those times had been different—his plane had been in good working order.

He checked the oil pressure once again and was heartened to see it was holding for the moment. There was obviously a leak, but maybe it wasn't as bad as he feared.

If he could get the plane down without damaging it, he had enough tools to make some repairs. He mentally inventoried what he had stowed in back—his camping equipment, his AM-FM radio, and the food supplies he'd planned to take to Mexico. It could be worse. All he needed to do was find a place to land.

There it was. He sent up a prayer of thanks. He'd spotted a meadow, lightly dotted with aspen, but relatively clear of the larger pines that would put a quick end to a forced landing. Then he glanced at the oil pressure gauge. Once again it was dropping.

He no longer had a choice. He had to put it down.

"This is it. We're going in."

His deep voice echoed in the small compartment. How could he sound so calm? Paige wondered if this was the time her life should be rapidly flashing across her mind. If so, her thoughts weren't cooperating. All she could think about was her father. Was he still alive? How was she going to reach him? What would the shock of her not arriving do to him? If only she knew his condition.

Her last conscious thought was: *There was so much I still wanted to do in life...*

Two

____

Paige groaned.

Icy water trickled down her face. She shifted, and a sharp pain shot through her head. *Is this what a hangover feels like?* she wondered fuzzily. *But I don't even drink.*

Other sensations seeped into her consciousness. She was moving, but not under her own power. The steady thudding that accompanied the pain in her head was coming from the hard wall pressed firmly against her right ear. Steel bands were strapped around her shoulders and knees. She tried to raise her head, but blackness engulfed her once again.

Minutes later, or maybe hours, Paige felt as though she were being held captive by miniature natives, only inches tall. Several held her head while their friends took turns beating on it with their minuscule hammers. Why wouldn't they leave her alone?

She attempted to raise her hand to her head, only to find it firmly tucked under a cover. At least they hadn't tied her down. If she could only free her hand, she could fight them back. One arm swing should swat them away like flies. But they certainly carried a mean wallop to be so small.

"You need to lie still, Paige. You're going to be all right...try to rest."

Where had she heard that voice before? The deep, warm tones comforted her. They were much deeper than her father's voice. Her father.

"Dad!" She tried to sit up. Where was he? He'd needed her for something. What was it?

"It's all right, honey. We'll get you to your father yet." The voice held a quiet authority that soothed her. Who was it?

An arm slipped under her shoulders and brought her forward. The movement caused the sadistic natives to double their efforts. "Please stop," she murmured, wondering if they spoke English.

"I'm sorry, but you'll be more comfortable without these wet clothes."

She wanted to explain that she wasn't talking to the quiet voice murmuring in her ear. It was those blasted natives practicing their construction skills on her defenseless head. But it took too much effort to explain.

A cool wet cloth gently touched her forehead, and she sighed with pleasure. Never had anything felt so good. Soothing strokes bathed her face and a gentle hand pushed her thick hair from her face.

"You have a slight concussion, Dr. Winston, but I don't think it's too bad. I'm sure you'll feel better by morning."

I hope, Hawk silently added.

He sounded so confident that Paige drifted into a natural sleep, content to wait for relief. Maybe the natives had been scattered when she sat up. Serve them right. They were insufferably rude.

Paige shifted in her sleep. At least she attempted to shift, but couldn't move. What was wrong with her? She opened her eyes and decided she had finally flipped over the edge of sanity into a surrealistic existence.

Nothing made sense. Her head rested on a hard, bronzed surface that moved gently. Her body rested comfortably against something large and warm. A canvas surface seemed to surround her, but it was hard to tell in the gloom. Was it night or day?

She attempted to raise her head, relieved to discover her tiny torturers must have given up and gone home, leaving her head with a dull ache. Her pillow shifted, and she focused fuzzily on a pair of black eyes a few inches away staring at her with concern.

What beautiful eyes, she thought dreamily.

"How do you feel?" the man asked, his voice rumbling in his chest. She realized her head had been resting on his shoulder.

"Like I should never have had that first drink," she admitted, and wondered why he chuckled.

Paige discovered she was lying entwined with a man with gorgeous black eyes. *So this is what my subconscious is up to when my back is turned. It has me in bed with a beautiful specimen of virile manhood the minute I slip over the edge. Interesting.* She wondered how long she would be in this condition, but decided she might as well enjoy it while she was there.

Paige discovered her hand draped across his bare chest and she tentatively moved her fingers. They worked. She could feel the warmth of his skin under the sensitive pads of her fingertips. She brushed her hand over his chest and smiled. *Not bad. Not bad at all.*

Other sensations began to impinge on her. She was cozily curled along the man's side, both of his arms wrapped around her. One of her legs was neatly tucked between his, her thigh nestling intimately against him. A warm tide of embarrassment swept through her. Never had one of her dreams been so vivid. Not only could she feel the steady beat of his heart beneath her palm, his soft breath felt like a feather rhythmically brushing against her forehead.

Paige knew that all she needed to do was roll over and look at her clock to come out of it, but she couldn't resist the temptation to enjoy the dream for another few moments.

She absently noted that the only thing each of them had on were their briefs, and yet she was quite warm. The covers fit snugly around them. She raised her head slightly and discovered they were in a sleeping bag.

A sleeping bag? Now where did her subconscious come up with that one? She'd never been camping in her life. The outdoors was a total mystery to her and, as far as she was concerned, would remain that way.

Oh well, a dream was a dream, and she obviously had no control over what was put in it. But a sleeping bag, of all things!

The man shifted slightly, and her thoughts flew back to him. Had his breathing changed? Had his arm tightened around her? His heartbeat had definitely increased.

Then she realized what was happening and jerked her leg away from him. *Okay, time to wake up now. We know what kind of dream this could turn into.* Paige tried to sit up, but was hampered by the man and the covers.

She blinked her eyes, trying to focus on the clock sitting on the nightstand beside her bed. She couldn't even find the nightstand. When she forced herself into a sitting position, the top of her head brushed against canvas.

An ominous feeling suddenly gripped her—a very ominous feeling.

She wasn't dreaming. She was definitely awake, but nothing made sense.

Paige tried to recall the reason why she was there, and the dull throbbing in her head increased its rhythm. She felt along her temple and discovered a large bump just below her hairline.

Panic began to course through her. She searched her memory for her name. Paige Winston. Her age? Thirty. Her occupation? Pediatrician. Her address? Thirteen-twenty-eight La Donna Drive, El Paso, Texas.

So far, so good. *Just take it easy. You've suffered a blow to your head and you're obviously disoriented.* Her medical training was striving to take over and be objective, but she could feel her heart slamming against her chest and she was breathing in short, panting breaths.

Now, then. The next step is to figure out where you are. She gazed around the small area enclosed by canvas, searching for clues. Nothing looked familiar.

Slowly she turned around and stared at the man still lying next to her. She was positive she'd never seen him before in her life. "Do I know you?" she asked politely, a tentative smile hovering on her face.

Hawk blinked in surprise. After only a few hours of sleep, his brain felt sluggish and he wasn't prepared for his passenger's unexpected question. He leaned up on his elbow, his muscled arm flexing painfully where her head had rested for the past several hours.

"Don't you remember?"

That question had to rank as one of the most stupid ones of all times, she decided in disgust. Why else would she have asked? "Didn't anyone ever tell you it's impolite to answer a question with a question?" Paige grumbled. She studied his face for a moment. She did not know this man. Of course she didn't. In which case, she needed to understand why they were in a sleeping bag together under some sort of canvas cover.

She rubbed her aching head, vaguely remembering the constant pounding from the night before. She wondered if this were what a hangover felt like. If so, she knew she'd made the right decision years ago when she decided not to drink.

Hawk watched her in concern. Her concussion must be worse than he'd first thought. He slipped his forefinger under her chin and slowly turned her head until he could see her eyes. Yes, they were definitely dilated. At least the right one was, which wasn't surprising considering the large knot on her temple.

Now what? He had done the best he could last night after they landed. He'd found makeshift shelter for her under the trees until he could unload the plane, set up the tent, and spread out the bedroll. His fear for her had galvanized his actions. He'd never forget the relief he felt when she had come to, even if it had only been for a few minutes.

"Do you remember anything about last night?" he asked, noting her puzzled expression with concern. "Do you remember the plane going down?"

She stared at him in bewilderment. A plane? He was asking about a plane going down.

Paige recalled watching a television news report of a jumbo jet crashing at the end of a runway, going up in smoke and flames. When had she seen that?

Paige rubbed her head thoughtfully. "I don't think so," she finally admitted softly.

Now what? Hawk wondered. Was there any reason to feed her fears by admitting that although they had made it down safely, the plane was in no condition to fly out under its own power?

"It doesn't matter." He edged away from her in the confined bed. "I've got to look for some dry wood to get a fire going. Are you going to be all right if I leave you for a few moments?"

His anxious gaze confused her. What was the matter with her brain? Her thoughts seemed to be sloshing around in some kind of gooey liquid, refusing to form any reasonable shape or make any kind of sense. She couldn't understand what she was doing here when she should be waking up in her own bed, in her own home, and getting ready to go to the clinic.

Hawk couldn't help it. Her anxious frown as she sat in the curve of his arm, the covers modestly tucked around her breasts, leaving her silky-soft back open to his appreciative view, was too much for him to ignore. He pulled her back down to him with some vague idea of trying to comfort her. "It's going to be all right, honey. Please don't worry. I won't let anything happen to you." He leaned over and touched his lips gently to hers.

As kisses go, his was far from demanding. It was almost soothing, and she relaxed in his arms, enjoying the sensation of being held and comforted.

She *had* to be dreaming. There was no other explanation. Maybe it was a dream within a dream, but she'd never dreamed of anyone who looked like him before. His kiss took her breath away.

Hawk pulled away from her slightly, surprised at his actions. He'd only meant to console her, and he found her warm response unexpected.

He forgot who they were and why they were there as, once again, he leaned down and kissed her. Her mouth parted slightly, unconsciously inviting his intimacy. She tasted so sweet, so warm and loving. Hawk soon lost himself in exploration.

What is happening to me? Paige wondered. Never had she felt this way before. Never had a man affected her so.

Who was he?

Paige stiffened and pulled away from him while she studied his features for a clue to his identity. She saw thick black hair that fell across his broad forehead; high cheekbones and rich skin tones; and magnificent black eyes that mesmerized her.

But who was he? And what were they doing in a sleeping bag together? They certainly weren't strangers to each other!

Maybe the bump on her head had been worse than she thought. What if she were more than just disoriented? What if she were suffering from some form of amnesia?

Paige closed her eyes and tried to blot out her surroundings. *Relax. Stay calm. Everything's going to be all right. Don't panic. Try not to panic your companion. He doesn't need to know how little you can remember. Maybe it will all come back to you in a few minutes.*

She opened her eyes and found herself staring deeply into his. "Were we in a plane crash?"

His well-shaped lips formed a small smile. "Not exactly. I was forced to land in a meadow last night."

"Oh." She continued to study him. He was so close she could see her reflection in his eyes. At least she'd learned something about him. He was a pilot. "Where are we?"

He shifted restlessly, moving slightly away from her. "Somewhere in eastern Arizona."

Arizona! What in the world are we doing in Arizona?

None of this made sense. How much of her life had she forgotten?

Paige rubbed her forehead. The pain made her feel as though her head were expanding with each heart beat. She tried to swallow, and her throat felt as though it had experienced a six-month drought. "May I have a drink of water, please?"

Hawk stared at her. Surely, as a doctor she should know a person with a concussion shouldn't have liquids. That was basic medical knowledge. *But she's not a doctor at the moment,* he reminded himself. *She's more of a patient. You can't expect her to diagnose and treat herself.*

He ran his hand down the side of her head, brushing the hair away so that it fell in long waves down her back. "I'm afraid I can't give you anything to drink,

Paige." She stared at him in bewilderment. "I think you have a concussion. You mustn't drink anything."

Of course not, she thought. *I know that. I've treated several children with mild to severe concussions. But I had no idea what one felt like.*

I've got to get out of here, Hawk prodded himself. He didn't know what he'd been thinking of, kissing her like that. If only she hadn't looked so bewildered and vulnerable. A strange feeling had swept over him—a need to protect her. *If I don't watch it, the only protection she'll need is from me!* He threw back the cover and reached for his Levi's.

The tent was too small for him to stand up. He wriggled the pants over his long legs, then threw the tent flap open and crawled out. It was still raining.

Swell.

That was all they needed. The storm from the night before appeared to be a forerunner of more to come. He glanced around as he slowly stood up. The sky was heavily overcast, and he wondered how he was going to get word where they were to anyone.

He had flown off course yesterday, trying to get away from the worst of the storm. No one would be looking for them in this area. There had been no response to his repeated calls on the radio. All he'd gotten was static. Somehow he had to get them some help. But how and from where?

He watched the rain beat a monotonous rhythm around him. He was going to have a hell of a time finding wood dry enough to burn.

While he uncovered small limbs and peeled bark from larger ones, Hawk organized his thoughts and sought solutions.

He and the doctor were fortunate in one respect—they had plenty of food and camping equipment, enough to survive for a few weeks at least. He glanced back at the tent, nestled along the edge of a sheer cliff towering above the meadow. It looked as though he and his attractive passenger might be camping there for a few days.

He didn't see how she would be able to reach her father anytime soon. Now that he thought about it, he realized that she hadn't even mentioned her father this morning, which was surprising. Could it be possible she didn't remember why they were flying to Flagstaff? Or did she even remember where they'd been going?

Hawk had seen more head wounds over the years than he wished, and he knew they caused unpredictable consequences. Paige appeared confused and disoriented, and apparently suffered from some form of memory loss. He could think of nothing that he could do for her in that respect. He knew very little about her.

Glancing around the meadow, Hawk was somewhat reassured about their situation. If they had to be marooned somewhere, he'd at least found a location that offered comfortable accommodations.

Uncertain about the possibility of flooding, Hawk had set up camp on the hillside overlooking the meadow and stream that cut through its center. The tent was almost hidden among the boulders and trees, but spotters could see his plane if they flew over.

He winced at the thought of his plane. The damage had been considerable, but any forced landing that could be walked away from was considered an unqualified success.

Only, Paige hadn't walked away. Once again he saw her as she'd been last night. She'd been wearing her hair in some sort of topknot on her head, but it had come down, its mahogany-colored length falling around her shoulders and down her back. Her delicate features and fair complexion emphasized her vulnerability, and he could still taste the fear that had threatened to engulf him when he'd discovered her unconscious. Never had he seen a more beautiful sight than when her eyes slowly opened to reveal their navy-blue color.

Hawk faced the situation head-on. He'd been strongly attracted to her from the first moment he saw her. How else could he explain his insane impulse to kiss her? She'd looked so bewildered—so beautiful— and he'd spent the night holding her in his arms, praying she would be all right. But he would have to ignore his reaction to her. What he had to do was take care of her and get them out of there.

He stared up at the sky. There was a real possibility they wouldn't be spotted anytime soon, in which case their only choice would be to wait until Paige regained her strength, then consider their options. They might have to hike out of the mountains.

In the meantime he might as well try to relax and enjoy their forced camping trip. They certainly weren't in a life-threatening situation as long as Paige continued to show signs of improvement.

The fire finally caught, and Hawk relaxed a little. He would have to make certain he didn't let it go out, after all the trouble he'd had getting it started. He straightened and went over to his box of provisions. At last he could make some coffee.

Hawk heard a movement behind him and turned around in time to watch Paige crawl hesitantly out of the tent. She wore the tailored suit and high-heeled shoes she'd had on the day before.

She stood in front of the tent staring around the clearing with bewilderment. Hawk realized she was swaying, and he dashed over to her.

"Paige, honey, you shouldn't be out of bed." He coaxed her back into the tent. "You need to lie quietly and give your head a chance to heal." She docilely sat back down on the sleeping bag. "The last thing we need is for you to get chilled." Hawk knelt beside her and hurriedly unbuttoned her blouse. "Your clothes are still damp," he explained as he unzipped her skirt and slid it down her legs. Her shoes came off last, leaving her in a lacy half slip and bra. He knew she'd be more comfortable without the constriction across her chest but didn't want to upset her by removing anything more. Hawk tucked her into the bedroll once more.

"Please stay in bed today, all right?"

She nodded her head, looking up at him like a trusting child. He found the cloth he'd used the night before and moistened it with water from his canteen. Gently he placed it on her forehead.

"What's your name?"

Her dark blue eyes continued to watch him. He felt his heart make a convulsive leap in his chest. So she still didn't remember him. Not a good sign. She didn't appear to be upset, just confused. The important thing for him to keep in mind was that she mustn't get upset. Perhaps it was just as well she couldn't recall much at the moment. As long as she didn't remember her father's illness on her own, he saw no reason to upset her with the news under the present circumstances.

He brushed his knuckles across her cheek. "My name is Hawk."

"Hawk?"

"That's right."

"So you're a hawk. I've wondered where a hawk lives. Now I know." Her voice had a little-girl quality, nothing like her normal husky tone. "He lives high in the mountains, in a rainy glen, hidden away from the troubles of the world." Her eyes drifted closed. "I'm glad I'm a hawk, too."

He sat there by her side most of the day, only leaving for short periods of time—to try the radio in the plane again, to make something to eat for himself. He made sure she didn't sleep too long at a time and listened for any sound that might mean someone was looking for them.

The hours passed slowly while he made his rounds between the fire, the plane and the tent. Toward evening the rain stopped and he hoped the clearing skies would bring help, but by nightfall there was no sign of rescue.

Three

——

Paige dreamed of soaring in the sky, dipping and swooping down through mountains and valleys and over bubbling springs. Sometimes she was alone. Other times a beautiful hawk flew next to her. A hawk with luminous black eyes.

She was hot. Paige pushed against the covers, but they wouldn't move. She tried to sit up and couldn't. Her eyes reluctantly opened, but it was too dark to see anything.

Where am I? she wondered in confusion. Mental pictures flashed across her mind of a man—a campfire—rain dripping from the trees—a tent.

That was it. She was in a tent. She tried to move again and recognized the hard surface at her back was warm, and breathing. She was curled up with a man.

She didn't know any men on that basis. So what was she doing there?

Her head hurt, but nothing like it had been hurting. She rubbed along her temple and felt the large bump there. That's right. She'd got hit on the head. But how? And when?

A large, muscular arm rested across her waist, keeping her snug against the man who shared her bed. *This is a sleeping bag...I remember now. I'm camping with this man. What did he say his name was?*

She couldn't remember. While she concentrated on remembering—she knew it was imperative that she recall his name—Paige fell asleep once more.

Sunlight filtered through the open flap of the tent when Paige opened her eyes again. She was alone. Raising up on her elbow, she looked outside and saw sunshine. She also could see a man moving around a campfire and smell coffee brewing. It smelled wonderful.

When she sat up, Paige discovered that the horrible pounding in her head she'd experienced the day before was gone. Thank God.

Who was the man who had looked after her? She could remember him coming into the tent, stroking her hair, placing a damp cloth on her forehead, speaking to her, but it all seemed like something she'd dreamed.

Now, however, she had to face the fact that she was not dreaming. For some reason she was alone with a man she could swear she'd never seen before. Not only did they seem to be camping together, they were sleeping together. Why? She could think of only one explanation—she must be married to him.

Paige tried to concentrate, tried to find some memory regarding a wedding. The only thing she got for her efforts was increased pain. If only she felt better, she was certain she'd be able to clear the confusion in her mind.

He had mentioned a plane. She rubbed her forehead distractedly. She remembered nothing about a plane.

Could it be possible she was married? She recalled the intimate way they'd spent the last two nights. She could think of no other explanation. Perhaps if she explained her lack of memory to him, he'd be willing to fill in the gaps for her.

Paige stretched, pleased to discover how much better she felt now that she had some course of action. Surely her memory loss was temporary. She glanced at the man by the fire once more. *It would help if I could remember his name.*

The tent was almost stifling when Paige crawled out of the bedroll. She looked around for her clothes, but all she saw was a backpack in the corner of the tent.

When she opened it, she found men's clothing. Shrugging at the inexplicable details of the trip, Paige dug around until she found a bright red-and-black-plaid shirt. It was much too large for her, but better than nothing. She rolled the sleeve up until she found her hand hidden in the folds, repeated the process with the other sleeve, then hesitantly stepped out of the tent.

"Where are my clothes?"

Hawk spun around at the sound of her voice. His jaw dropped. Paige stood in front of the tent with one of his shirts on. The shirttail hung halfway to her knees in front, but the sides came up high on her thighs. He caught his breath. Her long, well-shaped legs could be the envy of a Las Vegas showgirl. His gaze wandered to her trim ankles and bare feet before he forced himself to meet her eyes. He really hadn't needed a visual reminder of what he'd held in his arms for the past two nights.

She looked as if she felt better and he needed to say something—anything—to let her know he was glad. His tongue, however, seemed to have disappeared.

He strode over to the stack of bags and provisions covered by canvas and partially sheltered by a tree. He picked up her small bag and returned to her side.

"Here you are," he said quietly.

Paige felt shy around him for some reason. She accepted her bag with a nod and disappeared once again inside the tent.

Kneeling beside her suitcase, she threw open the lid, only to stare at its contents with dismay. There were a couple of changes of underwear, one pair of slacks and a few skirts and blouses. A pair of low-heeled shoes were tossed in on top. Outside of her small bag of toiletries, that was all she'd packed.

Paige threw open the flap to ask where the rest of her clothes were and remembered she didn't know her husband's name. The situation was ridiculous and getting worse by the minute.

"Where are the rest of my things?" she asked when he turned around.

Hawk walked over to the tent, concerned. "You only brought the one bag, Paige," he answered with a slight frown.

She nodded, determined not to get upset. Glancing over at the fire, she said, "That coffee smells delicious. I guess it's being out-of-doors or something, but I'm starved."

He lifted her chin and looked into her eyes. They were much clearer this morning. Surely it would be all right for her to eat something. "I'll pour you some coffee while you get dressed. Breakfast shouldn't take long."

When she stepped out of the tent, Hawk smiled reassuringly. Paige's navy-blue slacks and long-sleeved pink blouse looked more appropriate to their present environment than her suit, and the low-heeled shoes were much more practical than high heels.

Paige gave him a hesitant smile and Hawk impulsively walked over and held out his hand to her, much as he would have to a shy child. She brushed her thick hair behind her shoulder and slowly reached for his proffered support. They walked back to the fire together.

Hawk was relieved to have the rain gone, although everything was still soaked. He threw a piece of canvas over a large rock and motioned for Paige to sit down.

She was weaker than she'd realized. Just the small amount of exertion she'd gone through made her head swim. Perhaps she'd take it easy today—maybe take a nap after she ate.

Hawk poured their coffee in silence while he tried to figure out a way to find out how she was feeling and what she could remember.

Paige accepted her cup and took a sip. *Ah, did that ever taste good!* She looked up and caught Hawk staring at her. It was no use. She couldn't remember anything about him and she might as well be honest before anything further developed between them!

"I might as well admit to you that I seem to have a problem." She glanced at him, then abruptly dropped her gaze to her cup of coffee. "I'm afraid the blow to my head knocked out a few rather important memories.'' She forced her gaze to meet his and was encouraged by the warm look in his eyes. "I not only don't remember your name, but I don't remember anything about our marriage."

Marriage! Alarms began to jangle in Hawk's head.

She nodded, determined to be completely open with him. "I don't even know what I did with my ring," she confessed, holding up her slender hand and revealing its bare condition.

Hawk stared at her, speechless. Where the hell did she get the idea they were married?

Then he recalled sharing the sleeping bag with her during the past two nights. At the time, it had seemed like a sensible idea. The first night she'd been in shock and he needed to get her warm. Body heat was the quickest way under the circumstances, and he'd stripped them both down and hurriedly placed her in the warm cocoon consisting of the two of them wrapped in a down-filled bed.

But what about the second night? Why don't you explain to her that you aren't married but that she's expected to share the only sleeping bag until you're rescued!

"Hawk," he finally managed to say.

She stared at him uncertainly.

"My name is Hawk."

"Hawk? Is that your last name, your first name, or a nickname?"

Her question surprised him. Few people asked, but then, few people cared. If she was somehow under the impression they were married, he supposed the question was understandable.

"My mother named me Black Hawk, but I took my father's name later. My legal papers state my name as

Hawk Cameron, but I seldom use anything but Hawk.''

She was quiet for several minutes, trying to assimilate the information he'd just given her. "Black Hawk is an unusual name."

He shrugged. "I suppose to most people. But to my mother, who was a Jicarilla Apache, it was a fine name, very honorable."

"How did your father feel about your name?"

"He never heard it. According to my mother, my father never stayed in one place very long. He'd been gone several months before I showed up." He stated the facts surrounding his birth without expression.

She sat there trying to dredge up a mental picture of his mother, but drew a blank. "Hawk," she experimented. *Hawk Cameron. Mrs. Hawk Cameron. Paige Cameron. Paige Winston Cameron.* Why didn't it seem more familiar? For that matter, why didn't *he* seem more familiar?

Paige could feel the slight pressure in her head once more, and she recalled her dream of the miniature natives practicing their skills on her head. "Not again," she murmured distractedly.

"What's wrong?"

"It's my head," she muttered. "It feels like hammers are being pounded on it from all sides."

Hawk stood up suddenly. "Why don't you go lie down again and I'll try to find something light for you to eat. You still aren't recovered."

Paige rubbed her hand across her temple. "Yes, I'm sure I'll feel better once I rest for a while." He followed her into the tent and helped her take off her blouse and slacks with brisk efficiency. It was only when he brushed his hand through her hair, tenderly tucking a lock behind her ear, that Paige experienced an inexplicable feeling of unease. "We *are* married, aren't we?"

He gazed into her troubled eyes. *She needs to rest, and she doesn't need to worry about anything.* Those were the priorities of the moment.

Hawk kissed her gently on the forehead, then straightened, pulling the covers to her chin. Making a sudden decision, he responded, "Yes, Paige, we're married. Try to rest now."

She smiled and closed her eyes. Hawk left the tent and went back to the food cooking over the open fire. *Okay, smart guy, you've got all the answers. What do you intend to do now?*

Hours later he still hadn't come up with a solution.

When he crawled inside the tent to check on her he discovered her gaze following his cramped movements. "There isn't much room in here, is there?" she asked softly.

"No," he agreed. "When I bought it I hadn't intended to share the tent with anyone."

"Have you had it long?"

He smiled. "For more years than I can remember."

"You must enjoy being out-of-doors."

"Yes, very much."

"I don't think I've ever been camping," she said uncertainly. "Or did you already know that?"

"No. But I had already guessed as much."

She shifted restlessly and he picked up her hand, letting it lie palm upward in his larger one. "Are you hungry?"

Paige couldn't get used to her reaction to him. Her skin tingled wherever he touched her. His warm gaze seemed to draw her closer to him somehow, and she had the strangest desire to wrap her arms around him—to be held in his arms.

She gave him a tentative smile. "A little."

"I'll bring you something to eat," he promised. "You just relax and I'll be right back." Hawk abruptly left the confined area.

What is she doing to me? he wondered in dismay. Her eyes seemed to haunt him. They were so expressive of her pain and bewilderment—and her wariness of him. *And why not? How can she be expected to remember a marriage that doesn't exist?*

As soon as she was stronger he'd tell her the truth. If they weren't found in the next few days they could make plans to hike out of the mountains. She'd be better able to handle the news about her father when she was stronger.

In the meantime, he saw no harm in fostering the idea that their trip was in the nature of a vacation. If it made her more comfortable to believe they were married, he'd allow her that fantasy. He'd just have to keep in mind their true status.

For some reason it was important to Hawk that Paige think well of him. Surely she'd understand the reason for his innocent deception once she remembered the reason for their flight.

Paige was asleep when Hawk returned to the tent with her meal. He decided to wait for her to wake up and stretched out beside her, enjoying the opportunity to leisurely study her.

He couldn't understand why all of his protective instincts were aroused by this woman. But she was like no other he'd ever known. Her clear, melodious voice seemed to gently flow through him, and he'd often caught himself absorbing its sound like the parched earth soaked up life-giving rain.

How ironic she thought they were married. No two people could be more different. She was well educated and obviously successful in her field. He, on the other hand, had learned about life the hard way.

Because of his inquisitive nature he'd picked up a considerable amount of knowledge during his travels—and he'd spent time over the years reading about subjects that fascinated him. But he knew he was far from the polished male that Paige was accustomed to.

"Why are you frowning?" Her voice startled him from his thoughts.

"I was just thinking."

Her lips curved into a gentle smile. "Ferocious thoughts, apparently."

He grinned. "Something like that. I'm afraid your meal is cold, but I thought you needed your rest."

She turned onto her side. "I feel as though all I've done is sleep. I haven't been very good company."

"I'm not complaining." He resisted the urge to lean over and kiss her. "I'll be right back with some hot food."

When he returned she was sitting up, pulling a brush through her tangled hair. He handed her a plate, then set a steaming cup down beside her. Once again he left, this time returning with another plate and cup.

They ate in companionable silence. Hawk was glad to see that Paige had a good appetite. Even her color seemed to be improved. Hopefully the worst was over.

"Hawk?"

"Hmm?"

"Could you try to help me fill in some of the blanks in my memory?"

He tensed. "Are you sure you're ready to start probing? There isn't any real hurry, is there?"

She sighed. "I suppose not. I just feel so stupid at the moment."

"It seems to me that's a very understandable reaction. I'm sure anyone would feel the same way." He took their plates and stacked them on the ground near the opening of the tent. "Why don't you rest for a while longer? I'm sure everything will come back to you in time—just don't push it."

"Thank you for taking such good care of me, Hawk."

He glanced over his shoulder and grinned. "My pleasure." His smile caused a distinct disruption to her normally steady heartbeat.

He crawled out of the tent, then paused. "Try to look at this as a well-earned vacation. Relax and enjoy it." He picked up their dishes and walked away.

Of course, he was right. There was very little that could be done. Either her memory would return or it wouldn't.

Paige couldn't help but wonder how long they'd been married. She found him very attractive and from a certain look she'd noticed she could tell that he felt the same way about her.

She smiled to herself as she curled up once again. *Not a bad reaction for a married couple to have toward each other. I must admit I've got darned good taste for picking a husband.*

Four

———

Hawk disgustedly climbed out of the plane a few hours later. Nothing. He could get absolutely nothing on the radio. He had even tried his portable, battery operated AM-FM radio and got nothing but static.

He jumped down off the wing of the plane and looked up at the mountains surrounding them. He wasn't surprised at the lack of reception.

Walking around to the front of the plane, Hawk winced at the damage. He'd hit a partially concealed rock after they'd touched ground, causing the left wheel to crumple. The plane had gone over on its nose, effectively demolishing the propeller and damaging the left wing. That was probably when Paige hit her head.

At least he hadn't ruptured the fuel line, so they hadn't faced the added danger of fire. He just wished he knew what had gone wrong with the oil pressure.

At least they had been lucky in some respects. The camping equipment had come through relatively unharmed and it was making their forced stay much more pleasant. Paige was as comfortable as possible under the circumstances.

Paige. His thoughts kept coming back to her. He had checked on her several more times since they'd eaten. She'd been peacefully asleep with a slight smile on her lips every time he'd looked in on her.

Why did she have to be so beautiful? Not to mention lovable. He'd quickly discovered she wasn't the typically spoiled beautiful woman. In fact, she seemed unaware of her looks. Where had she been all these years not to know the impact she had on a man?

He hated to be the one to break the news to her that her father was gravely ill—and that at the present time there seemed no way to get her to him. He could only hope she would regain her memory on her own.

Hawk started back toward their campsite. He could hear the small stream as he approached it. He knew that all mountain streams flowed toward larger streams that eventually became rivers. If he were to follow it, the stream would lead him to people who had settled near the rivers. People meant telephones and rescue, but he didn't know how long it would take. He didn't dare try such a venture with Paige until she was fully recovered.

It was time to go check on her, time to plan something to eat again, time to decide what to tell her about their sleeping arrangements. He could feel his body's instinctive reaction to the idea. He wished he didn't find her so damned attractive. Now that she was feeling better, he had no excuse to continue to share the sleeping bag.

The alternative was to be a gentleman and use the extra blanket he'd brought along at the last minute. At this altitude the nights were never warm.

He had to face it—his mother had not raised a gentleman. So where did that leave them?

"Hawk?"

His head jerked up, and he saw her standing by the dying fire. She looked adorable, standing there with his plaid shirt serving as a jacket. She had brushed her hair until it fell in rippling waves onto her shoulders and down her back.

Seeing her standing there looking so young and vulnerable affected him strangely. He wanted to hold her close and protect her from harm. He also had to fight a strong urge to make passionate love to her. Hawk could understand the second urge, but he couldn't understand his fierce desire to protect her.

He took his time walking over to her, trying to get a grip on his emotions. "How do you feel?" he asked, lightly brushing his hand across her cheek.

She smiled. "Much better, thank you." She had trouble meeting his eyes. "Hawk, do you know where my hairpins are? I can't find any of them."

He grinned. "There's no telling. They're probably strewn between here and the plane. But you don't need them."

She looked up at him in dismay. "Of course I do. I can't go around with my hair hanging in my face."

"You could always braid it."

She stared at him for a moment, then slowly smiled. "I suppose I could. Why didn't I think of that?"

He gathered her hair into both his hands, smoothing it, stroking the glossy waves. "I'll do it, if you'd like." She nodded and stood quietly while he plaited her hair into one long braid, tying it with a small piece of twine and letting it fall to her waist.

"You have beautiful hair," he said gruffly, stepping back from her. She turned around to thank him, the words dying on her lips when she saw the look in his eyes. They were blazing with intense heat.

She watched his mouth slowly lower to hers.

His lips felt surprisingly soft as they hesitantly touched hers, and Paige felt a ripple of feeling run through her body. His arms stole around her as though they had a will of their own and knew where they belonged. She felt a stirring deep inside her, a gentle awakening of sensations that she couldn't remember ever having experienced.

Hawk's kiss deepened and the intensity of his searching mouth seduced her into relaxing in his arms. Without a conscious decision Paige discovered she wanted to feel his mouth on hers, his warm, muscular body pressed intimately against her. She slipped her hands around his neck, bringing her even closer to him. Perhaps her mind had blotted out all memory of him, but her body reacted to him with sudden warmth and welcome.

His lips explored her face with gentle, loving touches. He seemed to be memorizing the surface of her face with his mouth—her eyes, the curve of her cheeks, the sensitive length of her neck. When Paige felt certain her knees would no longer support her he returned his mouth to her lips, seemingly starved for the taste of them.

As they kissed, Hawk loosened his hold on her, gently stroking her spine with his hands, learning the contours of her back and increasing the pressure until she felt almost a part of him.

Paige became aware of his body's reaction to her and knew what he expected—what he had a right to expect—and her heart seemed to stop beating in her chest.

No! Not yet! I don't know him. At least I don't remember. It's too soon. I'm not ready.

She turned her head from his seeking mouth and buried her face in his warm neck. "Hawk, please. We need to talk."

The sound of her breathless voice brought him back to his surroundings and what he was doing. Shocked at his intense reaction to her, he abruptly dropped his arms and stepped away from her.

"I'm sorry." His voice was a hoarse whisper.

She stared up at him, her eyes almost purple in their darkened state. "It isn't your fault, Hawk. It's mine. I'm so sorry our trip turned out this way." She backed away from him, watching his face as he stared at her, confused.

Paige tried to joke about it. "It must be tough to look forward to a vacation only to discover your wife suddenly doesn't know you."

"Don't..."

"I'm sure this is only temporary, but you see, I guess I'm still a little shy with you. I'm just not ready to..."

"You don't have to explain to me, Paige. I'm sorry I got carried away just now. You have nothing to feel guilty about."

His eyes glowed intensely, and she couldn't resist resting her palm along his cheek. "I wish we could pretend we just met and get acquainted all over again."

His breath caught in his chest. She looked so wistful, and so very vulnerable. Actually, her suggestion had considerable merit. They had to do something while they waited and he needed to keep in mind not to touch her. He could handle that. He'd better be able to handle that.

Hawk stepped back from Paige and grinned. "Good idea. Why don't we get something going to eat before dark and we'll trade the stories of our lives." He paused, uncertain. "Or do you remember any of the past?"

She gave him a puzzled smile. "It's strange, because I seem to remember who I am and what I am, but I can't remember who you are or what we're doing here together."

Hawk dug through the food supplies and found a package that could be easily cooked in a pot over the grill. Paige sat down on a nearby boulder to watch. She knew she needed to learn more about how to survive in the wilderness.

When he didn't say anything, she finally said, "I've managed to figure out that we are camping, but I don't understand why. Did I dream it, or did you mention something about a plane?"

He glanced up from his meal preparation. "We were in a plane that I had to land during a storm." He stared out over the meadow. "You can't see it from here. I'll take you down there tomorrow, if you're feeling up to it. Maybe you'll recognize something."

"Where were we going?"

Damn. I was afraid you'd ask that question!

The silence lengthened between them. Finally Hawk looked up at her. "Well, I had in mind a camping trip, but not exactly here."

She laughed. "No, I can understand that. So you were flying the plane. Is that a hobby of yours?"

"No. That's how I make my living."

"Oh." In a musing tone, Paige continued, "You know, it's hard for me to think of you as my husband." Embarrassed at the admission, she dropped her gaze to the fire. Finally she forced herself to look at him. "Have we been married long?"

Hawk shook his head but kept his eyes on the stew he was stirring.

"I didn't think so. Otherwise, I don't think I could have forgotten you so completely." She studied the lean build of the man kneeling before her. He looked tough, but surprisingly graceful as he prepared their meal with economical movements. She shook her head ruefully. "I'm having to eat a lot of my words. I always said I would never get married."

That statement brought his gaze up to fasten intently on her. She noticed his surprised expression and blushed. She could actually feel the warmth spread over her neck and face. It was a rather absurd remark to make to her husband.

She knew he needed an explanation. "You see, I grew up watching how unhappy my mother was, married to a doctor. My father was rarely available to take her places. She could never count on his being home at a regular time for meals. Mother ended up having to make a life of her own, independent of my dad. They loved each other, there was never any question of that, but the life of a dedicated doctor precludes a normal married life." She paused, studying him. "Surely I told you all that when you first proposed, didn't I?"

She looked like a young girl sitting curled up on the rock with her braid draped across her shoulder. He straightened slowly and walked over to her. His eyes were on her level and he leaned toward her, kissing her gently on her nose. ''No, we never did get around to discussing why you were still single when we met.''

Paige was having trouble with her breathing, a condition that seemed to occur whenever Hawk was anywhere near. ''Oh. Well, then I was extremely unfair to you not to have mentioned it.''

Studying the man in front of her, Paige had a hunch she knew why she'd never mentioned it. Perhaps she hadn't wanted to discourage him. There was something elemental about him that spoke to her. In some respects she felt as though she'd always known him and been a part of his life.

She realized she was sitting there, holding her breath, hoping he would kiss her again. Paige acknowledged to herself that she wanted his arms around her, wanted to feel his strong body against hers. All of her senses pressed to convince her mind that she must love this man very much to have married him. Why fight her reaction to him?

Hawk's hands came up to rest lightly on Paige's waist. His mouth hovered inches from hers. ''Are you ready to eat?'' he asked softly.

Her obvious disappointment at his prosaic words would have been laughable if Hawk had been in the right frame of mind. He recognized her reaction to him and it didn't help him at all—it only made his strong response to her harder to control. One of them needed to stay in control of the situation, and she had enough to contend with trying to recover from her injury. Hawk couldn't hold her responsible for the misunderstanding of their relationship. He could only try to keep the situation within reasonable bounds.

While they ate they watched the sunlight slowly creep up the eastern cliff overlooking the meadow and disappear.

Evening approached. Hawk became lost in his thoughts of what tomorrow might bring. Search planes should have found them today. Since he'd seen or heard nothing, he had to accept the fact that there was a good possibility they would have to come to their own rescue.

"Are you based in El Paso?" Paige's question startled Hawk from his reverie.

"Yes."

"How long have you lived there?"

"A little over a year."

"You said you were a pilot. Do you have your own business?"

"No. I have a friend in the air charter business, and I've been helping him get it started."

"It sounds like fascinating work."

"I enjoy it."

"I have a feeling we don't have much time to spend together when we're both working." She glanced out over the peaceful scene. "Is that why we decided to go camping? To have more time together?"

He didn't want to lie anymore, but Hawk didn't know what to say. Paige was taking their situation in stride, quickly adapting to the change in circumstances and her loss of memory. He could understand her need for answers, but he hated to continue the deception for any longer than was necessary.

"Paige, I know you're concerned about your memory, but don't push it. Most of your questions will be answered for you when you're feeling better." He stood up. "Why don't you try to get some sleep?" He picked up their dishes and began to clean them.

Paige knew he was right. She was still very wobbly, and the least amount of exertion seemed to tire her. She was surprised to discover how eager she was to learn more about this man. She had gone against a lifetime of strongly held principles in order to marry him. He had to be a very special person.

"Thank you, Hawk."

He looked up from building the fire for the night. "For what?"

"For taking care of me. For being so patient. I know all of this has been a strain on you."

He slowly came to his feet. They stood facing each other, the flickering fire between them. "You're very easy to care for, Paige."

She had an impulsive desire to fling herself into his arms and hold on to him, not a particularly sensible action if she was determined to keep some distance between them.

"I'm sure to feel more like my old self tomorrow."

"I agree. All you need is more rest." He looked down toward the meadow. "I think I'll try the radio again. Who knows? Maybe this time I'll get lucky." Hawk took a couple of steps away, then paused. When he turned around, his face bore signs of strain. "Don't worry about my disturbing you, Paige. I've got a spare blanket. I think I'll sleep out here by the fire."

She tried to see the expression in his eyes, but the light from the fire wasn't bright enough. "Don't you want to sleep with me?"

"That's not the point. You need to get your rest, and—"

"I slept very well with you for the past two nights. Why should I be disturbed tonight?"

"Well, I, uh, you don't know me and—"

"I don't *remember* you, Hawk, there's a difference. You've made it clear you don't intend to push me. Believe me, I appreciate that very much, but there's no reason for you to sleep out here in the cold when we can continue to share the sleeping bag. Is there?"

Good question. Is there? Can you continue to fight the attraction and your reaction to her? Hawk ran his hand distractedly through his hair. *What can I say to her?*

"If anyone's going to sleep with the blanket," she said, "it will be me. I see no reason for you to be uncomfortable because I don't seem to have my head on straight."

They stood there staring at each other, two strong-willed people whom circumstances had thrown together in a bizarre situation.

Hawk sighed. "All right, Paige. We'll continue to share the sleeping bag, if that's the way you want it."

She could feel a bubbly sensation within her which she tried to cover with a formal nod of her head. "That's the way I want it."

She watched him walk away from her, disappearing in the darkness. The dancing arc of his flashlight helped her track his progress down the hill until even the light went out of sight.

Paige shivered, realizing that she was alone. Hurriedly she turned to the tent, glad to have the light from the fire to help her find her way. Her thoughts kept returning to the man who'd just left.

I love him, she told herself. *I must love him or I wouldn't be married to him.* Paige found one of Hawk's T-shirts in his backpack and decided to use it as a nightshirt. She sat down and pulled off her shoes.

He was an easy man to love. She thought of his quiet manner, his knowledge of the outdoors, his kindness to her. She thought of his magnificent build, of his voice that made her feel as though a soft brush had been smoothed across her body whenever he spoke to her. Most of all, she thought of how he made her feel every time he took her in his arms. She was pleased with her choice of a husband. If only she could remember making it!

When she curled up into the sleeping bag, Paige hoped that when she woke up the next day, she would remember everything between them.

Hawk heartily hoped the same. On his way to the plane, he knelt beside the stream and stuck his hand into the icy water racing across the rocks. He tried not to think about the night and the enforced intimacy of their sleeping arrangements.

He'd tried. He'd even surprised himself. Paige was evoking too many unfamiliar emotions within him, and he didn't know how to deal with them. How else could he explain his chivalrous impulse? What had shocked him was the sincerity of his offer. He didn't want her to be uncomfortable around him. What he wanted was for her to accept him. Why? What in the hell difference did it make?

The tent was quiet when Hawk eventually crawled inside. Until now his camping gear had been perfectly adequate for the demands he made on it, but now he found himself wishing he'd gone for extra sleeping bags and a larger tent.

He shone his flashlight briefly around the area, careful not to send the full rays toward Paige. She was sound asleep. Good. She needed her rest, just as he needed his. He sighed, thinking about trying to sleep with her. The last two nights had been difficult. He was afraid tonight was going to be impossible, but he had to try.

She'd been through his things, he noticed. Not that it mattered, but he wondered what she'd been looking for. Was it possible she was trying to find out more about him? He looked at his clothes, tightly packed. Of course not. They would tell her nothing.

He sat down and pulled off his boots, pants and shirt. He carefully lifted the edge of the sleeping bag and smiled. She was wearing one of his undershirts, no doubt as an attempt at modesty. He wondered if she knew how fetching she looked in the soft shirt, her breasts impudently teasing him through the thin material with their provocative tilt.

He flipped off the flashlight, took several deep breaths, then eased his way down alongside her. The only way the two of them fit in the bag was for him to pull her into the curve of his arm and he reluctantly did so. She cuddled next to him as though they'd spent most of their lives sleeping together in that position.

Hawk sighed. It was going to be a long night. He tried to concentrate on the next day. He had to think of anything but the warm, tempting body lying so trustingly against him.

She stirred and murmured, "Good night, love."

His heart pounded in his chest. Was she even aware of what she'd called him? What would it be like to know he was this woman's love?

She said nothing more, and Hawk realized she was asleep. Yet even in her sleep she'd been aware of him, just as he was aware of her. His hand slowly stroked her shoulder, then down her side, where it slid into the indentation between her ribs and hips. She was so small—so delicate—and so precious. He pulled her closer to his side, then determinedly closed his eyes.

Five

___

Sparkling sunlight warmed the meadow in early-morning splendor. Tiny droplets of water clung to the tall blades of grass and multileafed bushes and trees. A young doe grazed by the stream, pausing to look around the glen for any sign of alien life. She noted only the natural inhabitants—a family of rabbits, a couple of noisy squirrels and a busy racoon, already about their day's business. A blue jay scolded a venturesome chipmunk, and a mockingbird mimicked the lecture.

After three days the natural inhabitants of the meadow had come to accept the unusual presence of the ungainly birdlike structure lying drunkenly in their midst.

Hawk stood on the knoll near the tent, absorbing the scene before him. The place had everything he had intended to find in Mexico, with one addition—the beautiful woman he'd left asleep inside his tent.

He rubbed the back of his neck ruefully. The sleeping arrangements may have become acceptable to Paige, but the forced intimacy was playing havoc with Hawk. Celibacy had never been one of his virtues, particularly when he was continually reminded of the condition by the constant presence of an attractive and intelligent woman. No one who knew him would believe his behavior these past few days. He had trouble believing it himself.

He would have to stay away from her—keep himself busy exploring and fishing. Under ordinary circumstances, that should be all that was necessary. He raised his arms high above his head and stretched, trying to get the kinks out of his back. Unfortunately, these weren't ordinary circumstances.

Hawk strode down the hill. He might as well start making plans to get them out of there as soon as Paige could travel. Glancing around at the cliffs, he decided the first thing to do would be to get up where he could see the surrounding area. Maybe he would spot something—some sign of civilization. If so, he could probably leave Paige alone for a few hours while he went for help.

With a definite plan of action in mind, Hawk felt more in control of the situation. *Someday I'll look back on this episode and laugh. I'll remember it as my closest encounter with matrimony.*

Paige reached for Hawk, her eyes opening when she couldn't find him. Confused, she sat up. The tent gave mute testimony that she was alone. Slowly Paige settled back into the covers.

She barely remembered his coming to bed last night, yet she knew he'd been there. At one point she'd awakened to find herself curled on his chest, her face buried in his neck. She smiled at the memory.

What a set of new experiences she'd encountered in the past few days. She'd never before spent a night out-of-doors, never cooked on an open fire, and never tried to stay clean with the help of water dancing merrily along in a small stream. She was surprised to discover how much she'd enjoyed it. Maybe the bump on her head had changed her entire perspective. She couldn't remember ever feeling so lighthearted, so eager to involve herself in something besides her profession.

Paige had a fleeting thought of her father. She hoped her being away wouldn't create too much work on the rest of them, although her father was always nagging her to take some time off. He believed in periodic vacations as a means of resting the mind as well as the body.

Vacation. What was it about the thought of a vacation that bothered her so? Not her vacation—her father's.

He'd been planning to go to Flagstaff, to do some fishing. Had he gone? Paige rubbed her head uneasily. The pain was never far away, it seemed, and it got worse when she thought of her father. How strange.

She closed her eyes and tried to relax. *Don't push it. Each day you're better than the day before. Relax. Think of something soothing and pleasant.*

Her thoughts drifted, eventually settling on a pleasing subject. Hawk. The name fit him. He seemed to be a part of the outdoors, in tune with nature.

She found him fascinating. Hawk didn't need to call attention to himself—he'd be noticeable in any group. His strength seemed to be an innate part of him, something he took for granted. She found herself watching him whenever he was in sight. He moved with the flowing grace of a large cat. His worn Levi's and multiwashed shirts emphasized his muscular frame, and yet he seemed unconscious of his appearance. He also seemed unconscious of her, treating her more as an acquaintance than as his wife.

Paige sighed, then brightened slightly as she remembered the night before. Hawk might be cool toward her during the day, but at night he held her as though she were part of him.

Was it possible they had quarreled? Perhaps the trip had been planned to draw them closer together. From knowledge of her own nature, Paige had a hunch the problem stemmed from her obsession with her work.

If only she could remember. Because if that were true, she'd need to use their time together to mend the breach between them.

Now that she was awake, she might as well get up. Throwing back the covers, Paige reached for her pants with a frown. They were so hot during the day, but what else did she have to wear?

Digging into her small case, she came up with one of her straight skirts. With a little ingenuity, she could alter the skirt into a pair of shorts, which would provide some welcome relief from the warm, sunny days.

Paige found her emergency sewing kit in her handbag, then sat down crosslegged on the sleeping bag and started ripping out stitches in the skirt. Her small scissors gave her the most trouble, but she finally managed to cut off some of the length of the skirt.

It was almost an hour later when she stepped out of the tent. Her newly-made shorts hugged the curve of her hips, ending high on her thighs. She wore a thin, jade-green blouse with the top two buttons open, the tail tied in a knot under her breasts.

Too bad Hawk isn't here, she thought with a grin. *I could announce to him that he's Tarzan, me Jane.*

The sun was already high in the sky, but Paige saw no sign of Hawk. Should she wait or go ahead and eat without him? She wandered down to the stream and washed her face and hands. Oh, what she wouldn't give for a hot bath, or even a shower. Camping certainly left out a few of the basic amenities she'd always taken for granted.

A shadow fell over her and she glanced up, startled. Hawk stood between her and the sun—and her stomach flipped over. The only thing he wore was a pair of Levi's, hung low on his lean hips, and a scuffed pair of moccasins. He could have posed for one of Remington's paintings.

His chest was wide and muscled, and her fingers twitched with the remembered sensations of touching him there. The muscles in his arms rippled when he rested his hands lightly on his hips. His skin glistened in the sun, and for a moment she thought it was from perspiration, but when she slowly came to her feet she realized he was soaking wet, water forming tiny rivulets through his hair and coursing down his neck and shoulders.

Her mouth felt dry, and she had to swallow before she could speak. Searching frantically for a light tone, she asked, "What happened, did you fall in?"

Hawk noticed with dismay Paige's new outfit, and he knew without a shadow of a doubt his willpower

was being tested to its limits. Once again she had her
hair in a single braid, and the thin blouse did nothing
to hide the jaunty tilt of her breasts. The sleek shorts
she wore merely emphasized the beautiful shape of her
legs.

What had she just said? He shook his head, and the
tiny droplets flew over them both. She backed away
with a laugh, her hands trying to shield her face.

"I'd love to have a shower, Hawk, but that wasn't
exactly what I had in mind."

She glanced up at him, her eyes sparkling, her skin
glowing, her smile causing his heart to pound in his
chest, and his feelings for her exploded within him. It
was at that moment that he knew he loved her. Hawk
had never experienced the emotion before; he had
never even come close, and he had no idea what to do
about it. He just recognized that what he was feeling
for the laughing woman before him was love, and it
was slowly driving him out of his mind.

"Are you serious about wanting to take a shower?"

The sun was still in her eyes and she couldn't see
Hawk's face clearly, but his voice sounded strained.

"Oh, yes. I'd love to be able to really scrub down
and feel clean."

He glanced at the towel and washcloth she carried,
items she'd found in his bag along with a bar of soap.
"There's a waterfall not far from here where you can
shower and bathe. Do you want to go now, or wait
until after we eat? The water will be a little warmer
then."

She glanced around the meadow, already cherish-
ing the area. Why hadn't she known of the joys of
outdoor living, especially if they included a shower?
She grabbed his hand. "Let's eat first. I'll show you

how much I've learned about cooking over an open fire." She ran ahead of him, pulling him laughingly behind her. Then she made a ceremony of brushing off a place for him to sit down so that he could watch her preparations.

"How's your head?" He studied her face and wondered if she knew about the five freckles that artistically decorated her dainty nose. Only the bruise near her temple marred the delicate softness of her skin.

Paige looked up from stirring the biscuit mixture she intended to bake in the iron skillet. "It's fine. Really."

"Have you remembered anything more?"

She glanced down at the bowl she held, then forced her gaze to meet his. "No. I'm sorry."

"You don't have to apologize. It's not your fault."

"Well, maybe not, but it certainly has put a crimp in our vacation together."

"Uh, Paige, I want to talk to you about that..."

"Good, because I want to talk to *you* about it as well!"

She placed the biscuits in the skillet, covering them as she'd seen him do, then started mixing the dehydrated eggs with canned milk. She learned quickly, he had to give her that.

"All right," he said quietly. "What did you want to say?"

Now that she had his undivided attention, she was unsure of herself. She'd been rehearsing what she would say, but it was different with him sitting there, half dressed, watching her so intently. "Well...I've been having some uneasy feelings about us." She paused, but couldn't bring herself to look at him.

He didn't respond.

"You mentioned that we hadn't been married long. From what I can tell, you're a very independent person." She glanced up at him and was surprised to see a slight smile hovering on his lips.

"That's very true."

She nodded. "So am I. I'm also opinionated and hardheaded." She waited, but he didn't comment. Their argument must have been worse than she thought! "What I'm trying to say is I feel there's something wrong between us. Did we have a fight about something?"

"No, Paige. That isn't it at all."

Okay. Now is the time to tell her the truth, painful though it might be for her. With calm deliberation, Hawk began. "I met you when you came to the air charter service and chartered a plane."

She looked puzzled. "Why ever would I do a thing like that? I don't even like to fly."

"You said you wanted to fly to Flagstaff to see your father." He watched her and waited for her reaction.

A sudden pain shot through her head. Paige absently rubbed her temple. Her father. Flagstaff. He had planned to go to Flagstaff on his vacation. Had he already gone? He must have. Why else would she be joining him? But why?

"If my father were in Flagstaff, I don't understand why I would go as well. We would be very short-handed at the clinic." She shook her head, bewildered. "It doesn't make sense. Nothing makes sense." She caught Hawk watching her intently.

"Hawk, how long have we known each other?"

Hawk answered her in a firm, deliberate tone. "We just met."

She stared at him with a mixture of horror and dismay on her face. Hawk waited for her to reach the natural conclusion. Only she didn't.

"I can't believe it. I eloped with someone I barely knew!" She stared at him in shock, but she was in no greater shock than he. That was not the conclusion he'd expected her to reach. It was not the conclusion that was going to help him out of the situation he was in. What the hell was he supposed to say to her now?

She sank down beside the fire and abstractedly stirred their breakfast. Almost talking to herself, she muttered, "I must have been under a tremendous strain. My years of constantly pushing myself must have been too much for me." She glanced up at him. "Was I by any chance running screaming down the streets when you first saw me?"

He started laughing, then shook his head.

"Will you be honest with me? I mean, give me a straight answer if I ask you something?" She came over and knelt in front of him.

At last, here it comes, and the charade will be over. Not before its time, he thought.

She stared at him in solemn concentration. "Did I ask you to marry me?"

Bewildered by her intense expression and the tension he could feel radiating from her body, he slowly shook his head no.

"Oh, thank God!" she said, and threw her arms around him in an expression of relief. Breakfast was forgotten for the moment. Hawk found himself flat on his back, with Paige staring down at him from her position on his chest. "Oh, Hawk, you had me so worried. I've never been interested in dating, or getting involved with anyone. I never had the time or inclination for flirtations or affairs. And for a moment I thought you were going to tell me I'd engineered our whole relationship." She stared into his dark eyes, seeing herself mirrored there. "I'm so glad you were crazy enough to propose to someone you barely knew—and so glad I was crazy enough to say yes!"

With those last words her mouth settled contentedly on Hawk's, proving once again she was a fast learner. She traced his lower lip with her tongue, her lips moving lightly over the surface of his firm mouth, while her hands gently explored the wide expanse of his chest.

Hawk's arms came around her. Somewhere in his deepest conscience alarms were going off, but he was obeying instincts older than his conscience. He held her to him, her body resting lightly on top of his, her breasts lying trustingly open to his view. His hand slid into the opening of her blouse, gently touching her. Her body quivered like an arrow finding its mark. He could feel his self-imposed restraints slipping away from him. She felt so good in his arms, just as though that's where she belonged.

Hawk smelled something burning.

He rolled, laying her on the ground, and leaped to his feet. Their breakfast was smoldering on the fire. He managed to rescue the pans, but the ingredients were past saving.

"Lesson number one, young lady. A cook never leaves the kitchen while preparing meals."

Paige lay on her back, breathless, and watched Hawk as he found more food and began to prepare another meal. While she caught her breath she tried to deal with the new information she'd just received. Staid, stodgy Dr. Paige Winston, the dedicated spin-

ster of the pediatrics ward, had so fallen out of character as to meet a tall, dashing stranger and elope with
him.

She wondered if her father knew about it. Exactly
how long had they been married? Could it be possible
they were on their honeymoon? Hawk would have
some more questions to answer—but not quite yet.
She needed time to think things through. Every new
bit of information unnerved her. Paige wasn't sure she
was ready to face what their relationship would do to
her settled way of life.

*I suppose Hawk didn't know how to tell me we had
just gotten married. That's why being married seemed
so strange to me at first. We've probably never even
made love.* The thought of the two of them making
love seemed to set all her nerve endings tingling.

She watched the sun glisten on Hawk's bronzed
back. *It will be up to me to change the situation. He's
made it clear he doesn't intend to touch me.* She smiled
at the thought that he was willing to wait for her
memory to return before initiating lovemaking. How
could she let him know that she'd built up enough
memories about him since they'd been there?

Paige trusted her own judgment. Whatever her reasons that had convinced her to marry him in the first
place were good enough for her now.

Hawk turned to call her over to eat and found Paige
staring at him with warm tenderness. He realized she
was still under the impression they were married. Their
situation was becoming increasingly explosive. The
safest course for them both was for him to tell her

about her father and the truth about them, and ask her
to forgive him his deception.

I'll tell her right after we eat.

Six

Only he didn't. Instead, Paige convinced him she felt well enough to go exploring.

"Do I have to put on my long pants?" She glanced down at her bare legs.

"Aren't you afraid you'll burn?" Hawk resolutely kept his eyes on her face.

Paige stared up at the sun for a moment, then shrugged. "I'd rather risk it than put on those hot slacks again." With a warm smile she added, "Perhaps we can stay in the shade."

When she smiled at him Hawk had trouble remembering his train of thought. "We won't leave the meadow, so you probably will be all right."

Paige looked out over the pastoral scene. "How big is the meadow?"

Hawk checked the fire, then started down toward the water. "I'd guess it's about a mile long, maybe a half-mile wide." He pointed downstream. "Not too far in that direction the area narrows into a canyon."

"Have you been that far?"

"Yes. I also climbed the ridge behind us, hoping I'd see some sign of civilization. But no luck."

They crossed the stream, and Paige walked over to the plane. It was the first time she'd been up close to it. She studied it thoughtfully. It didn't look at all familiar. She tried to picture herself in it, but couldn't. Flying wasn't one of her favorite things to do. It was ironic she'd married a pilot.

Paige found the view from the valley very appealing—so peaceful and untouched. She felt as though she and Hawk were the only two people on earth.

A sudden thought occurred to her. "There must be a radio in the plane. Have you been trying it?"

Hawk nodded. "I've been trying it for days, but can't pick up anything."

"Do you think anyone will find us?"

"I'm beginning to have my doubts. They would have located us by now, I'm afraid."

"What if nobody finds us?"

"We'll have to hike out of here."

"When?"

He looked up in the sky as though waiting for divine guidance. "I'm not sure. If I were alone I'd leave today, but I don't think you're ready to try it."

"Why not?"

"Because you're still not recovered from that knock on your head." He glanced down at her shoes. "And I'm concerned that you don't have the proper shoes or clothes to take the strain of a trip like that. From what I could see, the going won't be easy."

"So we sit and wait."

"For a while, yes."

"I don't mind. I'm really enjoying the vacation. I just feel guilty being away from the clinic. But it's too late to worry about it. I must have made some sort of arrangements before I left."

Hawk was silent. He didn't know what to do about her continued loss of memory. On the one hand, so long as she thought they were married and this was only a slight alteration of their original plans, Paige was relaxed. Getting upset would be the worst thing for her.

Learning that her father had suffered a heart attack would be a tremendous shock to her, he knew. It was obvious the two of them were very close. She would be frantic to get out of there.

He glanced toward the end of the meadow and wondered how long it would take them to find help. She might be able to take a day's hike, if they took it easy. But what if it took several days, even a week? He hated to take the risk.

"How about my showing you that waterfall I told you about?" Hawk waited for her to join him by the stream before he added, "Would you like to take a shower now?"

"Would I? Just lead the way."

They returned to the tent and gathered up towels, soap and Paige's shampoo, then started down the hill once more.

Hawk led the way, Paige content to follow and enjoy the scenery. A slight path showed through the grass along the stream, and Paige realized Hawk had been along there enough to leave a faint trail. It wound along beside the water, skirting boulders and trees, but always returned to follow the stream wherever possible.

Paige heard the sound of rushing water before she saw it. A large overhang, part of the hillside that appeared to have been eroded by the elements, jutted out over the stream, hiding the waterfall from sight.

Hawk took Paige's hand and helped her over the rocks and dirt that had formed a blockade of sorts to their passage. They paused when they reached the top.

"Oh, Hawk, this is beautiful."

From their viewpoint the waterfall still towered above them at almost a right angle to the previous course of the stream. The abrupt turn had formed a pool where the water eddied and circled before finding its way downhill once more. The sunlight caught the water in flashes of brilliant crystal. Paige could hardly wait to get into it.

She looked at Hawk uncertainly. She just couldn't go in while he was standing there watching her.

He glanced down at her and smiled. "I think I'm going to go a little farther upstream for a while. Why don't you stay here and bathe? I should be back in about a half hour or so."

Bless you for being so understanding, she thought. She nodded shyly and began the descent to the water while Hawk turned his back and started up the higher incline that created the waterfall.

The area near the stream was strewn with rocks of various sizes. Paige found one that was flat enough so she could sit down. She pulled off her shoes, regarding them with concern. The soft leather was scratched and scuffed. They'd certainly taken a beating during the past few days.

She slipped her shorts and shirt off, folded them neatly, then laid them in a stack. Standing up, she glanced around self-consciously before she stepped out of her briefs. Hastily removing her bra, Paige stepped gingerly into the water. The summer sun had taken some of the icy chill away, and it felt good.

Moving carefully, Paige waded toward the waterfall, eager to feel its freshness beating upon her. The bottom suddenly disappeared and she let out a yelp as she plunged in deeper. The sun hadn't had a chance to warm the depths, and the cold water caused shivers to dance across her skin.

Paige determinedly swam across the pool until the spray from above started falling around her. She felt for bottom and eventually found it. The water was up to her shoulders.

Since her hair was already wet, Paige went back for her shampoo and vigorously scrubbed her head. Never before had she appreciated the feeling of clean hair quite so much.

After thoroughly rinsing her hair, Paige swam over to the edge of the pool where it was shallow enough for her to stand and soap herself. Now that she was used to the water temperature she found it invigorating. *All the comforts of home.*

Aware of time passing, bringing Hawk's return near, Paige quickly finished and swam to the deeper water. She felt so good. Perhaps she could talk Hawk into taking her on up the trail. She waded back to the side of the pool where her clothes lay. Once again she glanced around shyly before grabbing her towel and briskly drying off. Within minutes she was dressed.

There was still no sign of Hawk, and Paige relaxed by stretching out on the large flat rock and turning her face up to the sun. She lay there with her eyes closed, listening to the sounds of the glade—the twittering of the birds in the trees, the slight rustling of the leaves as a playful breeze flirted among them—and slowly drifted off to sleep.

Hawk watched Paige from his position high on the cliff near where the water fell to the rocks below. He had given her plenty of time to bathe and get dressed—or so he had thought. But when he'd paused at the edge of the drop before following the trail downward, he'd discovered that Paige was at that moment stepping out of the water.

The shock of seeing her nude stopped him in his tracks. He'd undressed her in the dark the night they were forced down. His only concern at that time had been to care for her and to bring her body temperature up.

Now he could see her in the sparkling sunlight, her hair streaming down her back, her shoulders narrowing to a tiny waistline, her hips swelling in a gentle curve that he found utterly enticing.

She was already dressed and stretched out on the rock before he realized he'd been standing there watching her like some sort of Peeping Tom. *Is this what you're reduced to?* he asked himself in disgust. Thank God she hadn't seen him lurking up there as though hoping to catch her. He shook his head, trying to clear it, and started down the steep slope.

A cloud passed across the sun, or so it felt to Paige, and she opened her eyes. Hawk stood there, his shadow across her. She smiled, a sleepy, contented smile, and stretched. "That was marvelous, Hawk. Thank you for bringing me up here."

"No problem," he responded in a gruff voice. "Are you ready to go back?"

She sat up. "Not really. I managed to rest while I was waiting for you." She stood up. "Would you mind if we go up the trail a little farther?"

How could he deny her anything when she looked at him like that? Maybe it would help him to exercise some of his frustrations out of his system.

He held out his hand. "We'll go if you'll promise not to overdo it."

She took his hand and held her other one up in a pledge position. "I promise," she vowed.

Paige was enthralled with the variety of plants, birds and animals they saw as well as Hawk's knowledge of them all. He knew their names, and he knew what plants could be used for medicinal purposes. He seemed to be at home in that environment, and Paige found herself envying him his freedom.

Now that you're married to him, it can be your environment too, she reminded herself. She sighed in contentment.

The climb was more strenuous than Paige had anticipated, and by the time they reached the ridge overlooking the meadow her head felt as though the little natives were back, hammering ferociously.

Hawk took one look at her white face and swore. "I knew better than to let you come this far. Your headache's back, isn't it?"

"A little," she admitted. "I just need to rest for a moment. I'll be okay." She sank down on a rock and tried to let the view soothe her.

Hawk sat down beside her and gathered her into his arms. "I'm so sorry, honey."

She rested her head against his chest. His heart seemed to be racing. "It's not your fault, Hawk."

"I'm responsible for you, and I haven't done a very good job of looking after you."

"You've done an excellent job of looking after me. How do you think I would survive in the wilderness alone?"

"But that's the point. We shouldn't have to be camping at all."

She pulled her head back and gazed at him. "You never intended to take me camping, did you?"

"No."

At least that explained why she didn't have the proper clothes for camping. "You were taking me to Flagstaff to leave me with my father, weren't you?"

"Yes."

What could have happened to their relationship in a few short days that she would have run to her father and he would have made plans to go off camping without her?

She knows most of it now, Hawk thought. *Let her think we've had a fight, at least until I can get her to her father.*

"Do you think you feel up to starting back?" He deliberately lightened his tone. "It's always easier going downhill."

All she wanted to do was lie down, but first she had to make it back to camp. Paige stood up and swayed.

Without a word Hawk lifted her into his arms. She fastened her hands behind his neck, laid her head on his chest with a soft sigh, and closed her eyes. She felt tired, so very tired.

Hawk took his time making sure each step he took was firmly placed. Thankfully he found a more circuitous route back to the campsite that wasn't as steep as the way they had come.

He felt Paige relax in his arms and realized she'd fallen asleep. He pulled her closer to him. She looked like a child being carried to bed, and he felt his heart expand with love for her.

How could he regret their time together—regret the chance to get to know Paige? He glanced down at her once again. She still had mauve smudges under her eyes. Why had he allowed her to coax him into ignoring his better judgment?

Because you become melted butter whenever she looks at you with those wide, pansy-colored eyes.

They reached camp at dusk. Paige had not awakened. Hawk carefully laid her on the bedroll, then returned to the fire and made plans for a meal. Thank God they had sufficient provisions. They could stay there for weeks if necessary. Only Hawk knew he couldn't last that long around Paige without cracking under the strain of wanting to make love to her. His whole body ached, and only part of the pain could be blamed on the hike he'd made that afternoon with Paige in his arms.

Night had drawn its anonymous cloak around them when Paige joined Hawk by the fire. "I'm sorry to conk out on you like that."

Hawk smiled. "No problem. Feeling better now?"

Paige nodded. "I don't understand why the pain gets so bad at times. Whenever I try to concentrate—to remember—my head feels like it's going to explode."

He handed her a plate and a steaming cup. "The answer is obvious, doctor. Don't think. Don't concentrate. Let it come in its own time."

"That's easy for you to say. You don't have any missing gaps in your memory."

"What I'm trying to say is that worrying about it not only isn't helping you, it's actually causing more harm."

She was silent while she thought about what he said. She began to eat. He was right—as usual. They ate in companionable silence while they watched the fire flicker and dance before them.

"Have we ever made love?" Paige inquired abruptly, ending the silence.

Unfortunately Hawk had just taken a swallow of coffee. He choked. In a strangled voice he finally managed to get out, "What on earth made you ask that?"

"I've been thinking about everything you've said. You avoid discussion of our marriage as though it were a mistake. You've admitted we haven't known each other long, so we obviously haven't been married long, and for some reason you don't seem to want to discuss it."

Hawk stood up. "That's right. I don't. Have you finished eating?"

Paige looked down at her plate, surprised to see it empty. "I guess I have."

He took her dishes, then brought her cup back to her full of coffee. Sitting down beside her, Hawk took her hand in his.

"Paige, please drop the subject of our marriage. Forget it. It isn't important at the moment. What is important is for you to relax, quit probing and get well. We're going to be faced with hiking out of here one of these days, I'm afraid. You've got to be ready for that." He turned her hand palm upward and slowly traced her life line with his index finger. "I care for you very much and I promise that I won't ever do anything to hurt you. You're going to have to trust me."

"I do. I've already trusted you with my life. I just don't understand what went wrong between us."

"Nothing went wrong between us. Won't you accept that?"

"I suppose I have to."

"It would help." He stood up, pulling her up with him. "Go to bed now and try to get some more rest. Will you do that, please?"

Paige's gaze searched his face. He looked grim, almost in pain. She wanted to wipe away the look of strain, to hold him close and convince him that whatever their problems, they could work them out together.

"All right, Hawk. Whatever you say." She went up on tiptoe and brushed her lips gently against his. "Good night, love."

He watched her disappear inside the tent. Hawk picked up his coffee cup and for the first time since he'd been forced to land wished for something stronger to drink.

Hawk sat in front of the fire staring into the flames for several hours. Maybe he couldn't control loving her, but he could damned well control what he did about it.

He intended to do nothing. Nothing at all.

Seven

"After I left the Middle East, I was in Southeast Asia for about three years." Hawk sorted through his fishing gear as he talked. He and Paige were by a pool formed by a turn in the stream that ran through the meadow. Hawk was leaning on his elbow as he picked up weights and lures, then carefully separated them into the tiny compartments of his fishing tackle box.

Paige lay flat on her back a couple of feet away. She was enjoying the quiet sounds of the meadow, the shade of the aspen where they had decided to rest, but most of all, she was enjoying Hawk telling her about his life. "Were you ever in the military?"

He shook his head. "No, I did some work for our armed forces, but on a civilian basis."

She watched the leafy shadows form patterns of light and shadow across him. Once again Hawk had dispensed with a shirt, and Paige stared at his tanned chest with unconscious yearning. "Haven't you ever had a place you called home, Hawk?"

He stared off in the distance for a moment, sorting through his memories. "I was born on the reservation near Dulce, New Mexico. For the first fourteen years of my life, I lived with my mother. I enjoyed those years...took them for granted." He gave his head a tiny shake. "But my mother got pneumonia one winter, and died." His fist clenched, the only sign of emotion she saw. "There was no excuse for losing her. I don't think she cared if she lived or not. She felt she'd raised me, I suppose, and wasn't needed." The quiet ripple of the water was the only sound. "She was wrong...but I never had a chance to tell her differently," he finally said in a low tone.

"So you left," Paige guessed. "And you decided you didn't need anyone."

He glanced at her in surprise. "Why do you say that?"

"Because I've seen children react in that manner when they've lost someone close to them. It's a fear of allowing someone else to get close and perhaps losing them as well." She picked up a twig and traced the blade of grass in front of her. "It's hard to lose someone when you're so young. I was eighteen when Mother died of cancer."

"But you had your father," he reminded her.

She smiled. "Yes. He was there for me, and I'll always be grateful for that. He helped me through the healing process that follows grief." Paige was silent for a few moments, then added, "I'd like to think we helped each other." She glanced up at him. "Have you met my dad?"

Hawk shook his head.

"I think you'll like him." Her eyes sparkled as she took in his indolent pose beside her. "I *know* he'll like you." She wrinkled her nose at him. "You're just what the doctor ordered."

Paige rolled to her side and leaned up on her elbow. Hawk had finished with his tackle box and had sat it behind him. Now she lay inches away from him. He could smell the light fragrance she wore, the heat of the summer day enhancing it, mingled with the soft, evocative smell that was her. He took a deep breath, trying to ignore the messages his senses were giving him. "What do you mean?"

"You have to understand that even as a little girl I was always seriously determined to grow up to be a doctor. With that type of dedication, I refused to allow anything to distract me." She ran her finger down his nose. "Even boys."

"You mean you never dated?"

"Some. I went to all the school activities and dances, that sort of thing, but I just wasn't interested in involvement. I wanted to hurry and grow up—to get on with life."

"It looks like you succeeded."

"Too much, according to Dad. He says I haven't taken time to stop and enjoy myself along the way." She gazed out across the meadow. "I'm beginning to understand what he meant."

Her sigh of contentment reminded Hawk that he needed to do something about their situation. He studied Paige, lying so close beside him. Did she have the stamina to hike out?

Their time during the past few days had been well spent. Paige no longer seemed to be suffering from headaches and her energy level was steadily increasing. He wished he had some idea how far they'd have to hike to find help. He'd be better prepared to make a decision.

"Paige?"

"Hmm?"

"Do you think you'd be up to hiking out of here?"

She looked at him in surprise. "I guess so. Are you getting bored?"

He laughed. "No, as a matter of fact, I'm not."

She smiled, and his heart seemed to melt in his chest. "I'm glad. Neither am I."

"What I'm saying is...I don't think anyone is going to find us, so we might better start seeing about rescuing ourselves."

She stretched, raising her arm high over her head. When she brought it down, it landed lightly on his shoulder. She began to draw small circles on his bare flesh. "Are you sorry you ended up having to camp with me?"

Hawk could feel his body tensing at her touch. Dear God, how he wished she would remember the truth. *Do you, really?* an inner voice whispered to him. *Aren't you enjoying your time with her more than you've ever enjoyed anything in your life?*

He sat up. "Not really."

Paige grinned. "I'm glad." She sat up too, and rested her head on his shoulder. "Next camping trip I'll make sure to pack the right kind of clothes."

"Paige..."

"Hawk..." They spoke at the same time.

"What were you going to say?" he asked.

"Nothing important, really. I just wondered if you'd like to go swimming."

"Swimming?"

"Uh-huh. It's really warm today. You know where that waterfall is—where we've been showering. It's deep enough to swim, if you'd like to."

If I'd like to!

Paige jumped to her feet. "Come on. Let's try it— you might even like it." She laughed, a light, happy sound that was Hawk's undoing. He wanted this woman to be happy. He wanted to spend the rest of his life making her happy, but he didn't have the slightest idea how to do that.

She grabbed his hand and pulled him to his feet, leading the way while they followed the stream to the waterfall. The splashing water made a merry sound in the quiet of the warm day.

Paige immediately sat down and took off her shoes. It occurred to Hawk that swimming wasn't a good idea, but he couldn't seem to find his voice to explain why before she took off her blouse and shorts.

The tiny wisps of clothing she now wore hid nothing from view. Her skin turned a rosy hue as she determinedly met his startled gaze. "I don't know why I'm so bashful with you. After all, we *are* married." With a hint of defiance she unsnapped her bra, then stepped out of her tiny briefs.

The past few days had begun to tan her arms and legs, and her tan emphasized the ivory sheen of the rest of her. Hawk could only stare.

His gaze caused her blush to burn deeper, and Paige hurriedly lowered herself into the water. *How brazen can you get,* she admonished herself. *He's been a perfect gentleman, considerate of your condition, and you're flaunting yourself like some sex-starved wanton.*

But she wanted to let him know that her loss of memory didn't have to prevent them from enjoying their idyllic time together. His aloof attitude was no longer necessary, but she didn't know how to tell him. Hopefully he would understand that she was showing him.

She heard a splash behind her and knew that Hawk had joined her, but she didn't quite have the courage to turn around and face him. Instead, she swam to the side of the pool where they had left the soap and shampoo. She began to unbraid her hair, impatiently tugging at the strands. When her hair was free, she vigorously shampooed it, working up a lather, then stood under the waterfall to rinse it.

After diving under the water to make sure all the soap was gone, Paige came up face first, squeezing the water from her hair. Hawk stood a few feet away, watching her with such a tender, yearning expression her heart felt as though it would burst within her.

The water barely covered his hips. He'd followed her example and left his clothes on the large rock beside the stream. The sun on the water shot sparks of light all around him. The water glistened on his shoulders and chest, and Paige knew he was the most beautiful thing she'd ever seen—handsomely rugged, symmetrically formed, his face reflecting his love for her. *Of course he loves me, just as I love him. That's the best reason for marriage I know.*

She moved over to him, watching his eyes dilate as she approached. The water was much deeper on her, it stopped just below her breasts, so that they seemed to be floating. She didn't stop until she was touching him, her breasts lightly rubbing his chest.

"Do you know what I think?" she asked in a husky voice.

It was all he could do to keep his hands off her. He could feel the trembling throughout his body, and he knew that she was close enough to feel his reaction to her.

"No." He had trouble getting the short syllable past his dry lips.

"I think the reason I wasn't interested in anyone, and didn't want to get involved, was because I was waiting for you. Somehow I knew you were out there somewhere and that I'd know you when I saw you." She placed her arms around his neck, pulling her body against his. "I'm so glad I waited."

Hawk's strong self-discipline broke and his arms wrapped around her, pulling her even closer to him. His mouth found hers in a yearning kiss that held all the pent-up emotion he'd been fighting for days. "Oh, Paige, I love you so much," he muttered when he finally paused to take a breath.

She was having trouble breathing. "I love you too, Hawk. I feel that I've loved you all of my life."

The soft call of a bird sounded in a nearby tree, and an errant breeze whispered softly through the leaves. Hawk found her mouth once more and took possession, recognizing that it was time to quit fighting what was between them—knowing this was what he needed, what they both needed—and wanted. The world was light years away. They were in their own special paradise, just the two of them, and they were in love.

He could feel the flutter of her pulse under his hand where it rested lightly across her collarbone. His heart felt as though it would crack the wall of his chest with its heavy thudding. He could no longer resist touching her after all the many nights he'd lain awake, holding her, wanting her, determined to resist. Now his resistance was gone.

Paige felt his light touch shimmer down her body, tracing the curve of her waist and hips. She had never been touched like that and had no idea how much she would welcome it. Perhaps it was only his touch that could make her feel so loved and wanted.

Hawk became aware they were still standing in the small pool. He swung Paige up in his arms and slowly walked to the edge of the stream, his kiss possessing her. When he climbed out of the water he knelt on the grass that covered the flat area nearby, placing her gently on the ground.

His hand rested lightly on her ribs and slowly smoothed across her stomach, her abdomen, then lower. He paused. She was so delicate, so beautiful.

Hawk stretched out beside Paige, determined not to rush her. He leaned over her, his hair brushing against her shoulder while his lips traced a line across the soft swell of her breast. His mouth settled briefly on the darkened tip, then carefully caressed its mate.

A languorous feeling flowed through Paige, her thoughts seeming to float away like the soft wisp of cloud overhead. She could only feel. She felt the touch of his mouth so intimately pressed to her body; she felt his hand gently stroke across her thigh and hip. The moist heat of his body radiated his special scent and she found it heady.

Her tentative fingers tried to imitate what he was doing. He'd been her teacher all week. It was time for a new lesson—this time in the art of loving.

Her hand brushed down his chest and she felt the muscles of his stomach and abdomen. Her fingers lightly brushed against his arousal, and his whole body jerked.

"I'm sorry," she whispered.

"Don't be. It's just that I'm not sure of my control where you're concerned. You've tested it to its limits, I'm afraid."

She looked deep into his eyes and saw the love and desire within them. Her voice shook as she said, "You don't need to have control with me, Hawk. Just love me."

"I do. Very much."

Hawk began to show her how to express her love in physical terms, and Paige responded like a flower bud opening to the sun in full maturity. She had waited for years for this man and it scared her to think she might not have recognized him when they first met. But she had. She hadn't let convention, different life-styles, or different backgrounds sway her.

Now he was hers.

Hawk carefully lowered his body over hers. She was so small and he didn't want to hurt her. His mouth claimed hers once again and his hand gently brushed across her upper thighs. He pulled back slightly to see her face, to watch her reaction as he took her for the first time, but he hoped fervently, not for the last.

She lifted drowsy eyelids to gaze dreamily at him, and Hawk felt as though a giant hand grabbed his heart and squeezed. How could he make love to her while she believed they were married? How could he take advantage of what she felt for him without telling her the truth?

He cupped her face between his hands, his weight still on his elbows. "Paige, darling, listen to me..."

Her smile was heartstopping. "I'm listening. Is this where you tell me you're a virgin?"

He choked, a chuckle almost strangling him. "No, I'm afraid not."

"I figured as much. Most thirty-six-year-old adventurers I've met have the same problem."

How could she joke when everything was so serious? *But she has no idea what I have to tell her.*

"How many thirty-six-year-old adventurers have you known?" he murmured, unable to resist the temptation to kiss her once more. He tried to ignore how well their bodies fit together. He was so close to taking her, so very close.

She kissed him back. In a breathless voice she managed to say, "Oh, dozens I'm sure. I just can't recall their names at the moment."

"That's good. Oh, baby, you feel so good, and I want you so much."

"But you're afraid it's going to hurt me, aren't you? Please don't worry. If I'm willing, you shouldn't mind."

"Paige. There's something I have to tell you. I can't make love to you without your knowing."

His grim tone caught her attention. Then she realized how still he was, how full of tension. The lazy seductiveness of a few moments ago was gone. "What is it?"

"Paige, the day of the crash you hired me to fly you to Flagstaff because you'd heard your father was...ill. The plane went down a few hours later."

He could feel her stiffen beneath him, and he rolled away from her, coming up on his side to stare down at her. He watched the myriad emotions flashing across her face and he wished he could protect her from them. But it was too late.

Somewhere deep inside her Paige could feel the pain starting. Confused emotions darted at her from several different directions at once. Hawk was telling her they didn't know each other. He was telling her he was only a man hired to fly her to her father. He was telling her...

Paige sprang to her feet, frantically searching for her clothes. She spun around, hastily pulling them on, refusing to face the man who still lay where she'd left him, seemingly unconscious of his nudity.

When she was dressed she spoke without looking at him. "So this whole scene has been a complete farce. Not only am I not married to you, I don't even *know* you."

"That's not true, Paige. We may not have known each other when you hired me, but we've had several days together, and I think we've learned a great deal about each other. I know I've told you more about myself than I've ever told another living soul."

She finally forced herself to look at him, then flinched. He was making no effort to cover himself, a reminder of what had so nearly happened.

"Would you please put on some clothes?" Her tone was icy and his heart sank. She was taking it as badly as he'd imagined. But then, what could he have expected?

"Paige, I think we need to talk about this."

"About what? About the fool I've made of myself? That really isn't necessary. I'm well aware of it. The frustrated spinster finds the man of her dreams and decides she's married to him. That makes all those fantasies acceptable, doesn't it? I'm sure you've had a hard time not laughing in my face!"

"I haven't been laughing, Paige. I've been falling in love with you."

"Stop it! You don't need to continue the charade now. I understand. The only other thing I need to know is why I was flying to see my father. Surely you can tell me that. You said he was ill. My father is never ill."

By this time Hawk had pulled on his Levi's and stepped into his moccasins. He combed his hair back with his hands. When he walked over to where Paige stood, she backed away from him. He stopped, resting his hands on his hips.

"You told me that your father had a heart attack. That was why you were in a hurry to get there."

Paige felt faint and she sank down on the large rock where she'd had her clothes. The news was fresh to her, and the shock was every bit as severe as the first time she'd heard it. "A heart attack..."

"Yes."

"And you've kept me here all this time when I needed to be in Flagstaff!" Her voice rose in agitation.

He waved his arm. "Well, as you can see, I don't have a magic carpet that will whisk you away. Otherwise, I would have sent you right on."

"But why haven't we hiked out?"

"Because I thought you needed to recover. I didn't know if you had the strength and the stamina for what will probably be a very grueling trip." He dropped his hands. "I kept hoping someone would find us."

Distraught, Paige looked around the peaceful meadow. "You're an Indian. Why haven't you sent up smoke signals?"

"Very funny."

"I'm not *trying* to be funny. I'm trying to get out of this place."

"What do you think *I've* been doing?" he demanded.

"Seducing me."

They stared at each other in anger, in hurt, and in despair. Their paradise had disappeared, along with any dreams of a possible future.

Hawk stared at her for a long time, his face grim. Finally he spoke. "If I'd been trying to seduce you, Paige, we wouldn't be having this conversation. I would have gone ahead and made love to you." His mouth turned up in a sardonic smile. "You certainly weren't doing anything to stop me."

He disappeared upstream, heading away from their camp.

Eight

Paige didn't remember returning to the camp, but she found herself sitting in front of the tent. Their tent. They had spent several nights together, nights wrapped in each other's arms, nights when she'd wondered why he didn't make love to her.

Now she knew.

The pain had grown and blossomed within her until it seemed to consume her. Her whole body ached and she shook so hard it was almost as if she was undergoing a chill.

Shock. I'm in shock. My dad is ill. My marriage is nonexistent.

There was no Hawk in her life. There never had been—there never would be. Hawk was a mirage that had lingered longer than most.

He didn't make love to you. He could have. He knew it—you knew it. But he didn't. A sob escaped her.

How can I face him again? How can I pretend that nothing has changed? Everything has changed. Nothing will ever be the same. I can't face him. I just can't.

Paige glanced around the meadow. She remembered all she had learned from Hawk during the week. He'd pointed the way downstream that would be the best direction to go if they had to walk out. She hadn't cared. She hadn't wanted to leave. She hadn't known about her dad.

Oh, Dad, please don't die. I need you so much. Never more than I do now.

A growing determination seemed to grab her, forcing her out of her misery. She had to get to her father and she had to get away from Hawk. Standing up, she looked toward the stream. She didn't know where he'd gone and didn't care. He knew she wanted to leave here. She glanced around at the tent. There was no way she could stay there another night.

Once her mind was made up, Paige wasted no time gathering some supplies, taking the extra blanket and changing into her heaviest clothes. She wrapped everything she'd gathered in the blanket, then folded it as small as she could and tied it around her waist with some of Hawk's twine. It was bulky, but it left her hands free.

She stared up at the sun, trying to figure the time. She had no idea, but it seemed to be early afternoon. There must be several hours of daylight left. Perhaps she could find someone before dusk. It was better than sitting there waiting to face Hawk.

Hours later Paige wondered if she'd made a mistake. She was hot, tired and hungry, and the terrain had become increasingly rugged. The stream had left the pretty meadow and dropped at an alarming rate through giant boulders and tumbling rocks. She could no longer follow the waterway and was forced to fight through the underbrush, hoping not to lose track of the stream, the only guide she had.

Paige was glad she'd taken the time to rebraid her hair. It had snagged on an overhanging limb, but would have been so much worse loose. As it was, she felt as though a giant had tried to pull her hair out by the roots.

The soft mauve of twilight was touching the mountains around her when Paige slipped and fell, rolling down a rough incline until she landed in a heap at the bottom. Luckily she'd been deposited once again by the stream that had grown into an energetic river since leaving the meadow. She lay there, too sore to know if she were truly hurt or not.

Eventually Paige forced herself into a sitting position. Her clothes had saved her from abrasions but they'd paid the price with several rips and tears. She gingerly tested each ankle. They seemed to be all right, and she breathed a quiet prayer of thanks.

She looked around and discovered that she was sitting on a slight overhang above the river—not a bad place to camp for the night. She wasn't too far from the water, but far enough not to be bothered by any of the forest inhabitants who might want a drink. She hoped. Hawk had described some of the animals that lived in the area, most of which she'd only seen in a zoo. She would just as soon leave it that way.

If she were going to spend the night there, she needed to gather wood for a fire. With fresh determination, Paige limped into the underbrush, dragging out dead limbs. She didn't have anything to chop them up, but she had matches and she'd watched Hawk start a fire by peeling off the dry bark of the dead limbs.

He'd taught her a lot.

She sat back on her heels and thought about him. The hard physical exercise she'd experienced during the past several hours had taken away some of her emotional pain. In fact, she'd been able to identify part of the pain—pride and anger at being fooled. After all, he *had* lied to her. She had specifically asked him if they were married, and he had said yes.

She wondered why. What had he gained out of the charade? If he'd made love to her that first night, or any night afterward, she could better understand the lie. She shook her head. None of it made sense.

Once Paige had the fire going, she quickly pulled out the packets of food she'd brought, glad she'd decided to bring the small pot despite its bulk. She dumped the food in the pan, adding water, then watched it come to a boil. Never had she been so hungry. Never had she been so alone.

Alone. Paige had never really thought about what that meant before. She'd always been so busy with her life, snatching moments for herself to catch up on reading or writing, taking her solitary life for granted.

What if she were lost? What if she never found another person in all of this wilderness? What had made her think she could blithely take off and find her way out of there when Hawk had been hesitant to try?

She was a fool. Her pride and hurt feelings had compounded the problem, and now she'd taken an

action she couldn't change. She wasn't even sure she
could find her way back to the meadow, even if she
tried. And she was too tired to try. Her head was
throbbing for the first time in days, and she knew
she'd overdone it.

Hawk had been right. She wasn't strong enough,
and she didn't have the stamina—but she had to keep
going.

Tomorrow. She would get a good night's rest and
start out again tomorrow, and the next day, and the
next. She had food. She would stay close to the river
so she'd have water. She had a bed of sorts. She would
make it because she had no choice.

Hawk knew he had to return to camp and face Paige
sooner or later, but he wasn't looking forward to it.
The strenuous hike upstream had done him good. It
had helped to clear his brain of the fever Paige created within him whenever he was around her.

He hadn't realized how isolated he'd been from
people until Paige appeared in his life. Since his
mother's death, he'd never formed a close relationship with anyone. He'd never had any responsibilities
to anyone else; he'd never concerned himself over another person; he'd never felt protective toward another person—until Paige.

Of course she was upset. He'd spent the afternoon
thinking about how he would have felt in her place and
knew he'd have been mad as hell at the deception. He
hadn't really faced until now how hurt she'd be—or
maybe he'd been so wrapped up in what he was feeling that he hadn't given a thought to her feelings.

He'd hurt her, and she was the one person whom he
wouldn't have hurt for the world. He'd spent the

afternoon trying to figure out a way to ask her forgiveness, to explain his reasoning for allowing her to think they were married.

He'd also come to grips with the problem that had been eating at him for days. They had no future together. He'd allowed himself to live in the world created by Paige's misunderstanding of their relationship. He should have known better. She had her life, had even explained to him the heavy demands made on a doctor and why she never expected to marry.

He knew marriage was not part of his plans, just like they'd never been a part of his father's. It was bred into him; he was too restless to stay in one place for long.

So where did they go from there? What could he say to Paige? *I love you, but you wouldn't fit into my lifestyle, so it's just as well we aren't actually married?*

It was late afternoon when a grim-faced Hawk returned to their camp, determined to face Paige and be as honest as possible with her, only to find her gone.

He had no trouble reading the signs of her activity, and noted with unconscious approval what she'd chosen to take with her. Then the realization of what she had done hit him. She was going to try to make it out of the mountains alone!

"*Paige!*" His bellow echoed around the meadow, startling the small animals and birds. Of course, she couldn't hear him. He tried to determine how long she'd been gone. She must have left hours ago. He glanced up at the sun. He had to find her. He had deliberately omitted some of the stories that might have frightened her—that frightened him just thinking about her being on her own. Not all the animals in the

mountains were friendly. There were pumas and other
wildlife that were aggressive predators.

Hawk broke camp in his usual, thorough manner,
packing the tent and sleeping bag in their small cases
and stowing them on his backpack. He gave only
fleeting thought to his plane, wondering if he'd ever
find it again. Right now he had more immediate
concerns.

He started downstream at a slow trot, following her
trail.

Hawk found himself cursing under his breath, the
first sound he'd made during the past several miles.
From her tracks he could tell she was tired. Of course
she was tired. There was no trail to follow and the
rugged area where the stream fell to the lower slopes
of the mountain range was treacherous.

Daylight was fading and he still hadn't caught up
with her. The sensible thing to do was wait for daylight, then pick up her trail again. Not that he needed
to track her. She was staying as close to the stream as
she could. She must have remembered what he'd told
her.

Would she remember that he'd also told her he
loved her?

He knelt by the water and drank, trying to decide
what to do. He'd gained on her; her tracks weren't but
a couple of hours old. But could he keep going without possible injury to himself?

I can't sit here and wait, he decided. He dug into his
pack for a small flashlight and started down the incline. It was going to be a long night.

Hawk lost track of time. He didn't seem to be making much progress, and having to watch where he was

going by the small light was even more time-consuming. Then his luck began to turn.

The moon appeared over the rim of the surrounding hills. Thank God for a full moon. Within minutes the landscape was touched by a ghostly hue. He still had to be careful. The light could be deceptive, and he didn't need to step into a hole that he'd mistaken for a shadow.

He paused at the top of a long slope and spotted her fire. He hadn't realized how frightened he'd been for her until he saw the light and her small shape huddled nearby. Then his knees almost buckled with relief.

She was all right. He took his time coming down, taking care to place each foot on firm ground. He was over halfway down when he came to the place where she had fallen. The rocks and brush showed that she had rolled. His heart leaped, then settled painfully back in his chest. She had to be all right. Otherwise, she couldn't have set up camp. He could see that she had chosen well. Despite everything, he was proud of her.

Paige kept waking up, then dozing back off. She had built a large fire, not only for warmth but to keep any animals away. Hawk had assured her that most of the wildlife was more afraid of her than she was of them, but she didn't want to take any chances.

She lay there remembering how well she'd slept with Hawk. Already she missed him so much. Her wounded pride and bouts of self-pity were small comfort to her now. She wondered what he was doing. She pictured him sitting beside the fire in the meadow, watching the moon come up. It was beautiful tonight. Would he miss her? He was probably relieved to have her gone.

Paige cringed at some of her memories; she'd behaved like a wife in love with her handsome husband. Hawk had handled her so well. He hadn't encouraged her, but he had been careful not to hurt her feelings. He'd also told her he loved her.

She had a feeling he didn't admit that to many people. From what he'd told her about himself, he let very few people get close to him. But he'd been gentle with her, teaching her how to camp, how to read trail signs, how to fish. He'd been so patient with her lack of knowledge about his world. Would she ever see him again?

"Paige?"

She bolted upright, wondering if she were dreaming that he'd called to her. Glancing at the fire, she saw Hawk standing at the edge of its light. Or was it her imagination? She blinked her eyes, and when she opened them again he was striding across the clearing toward her.

"Hawk!" Forgotten were the hurts of the day, both physical and emotional. Paige was aware of only one overwhelming thought. She loved Hawk as she had loved no one before in her life. It no longer mattered that he had lied to her. The important thing was that he'd followed and found her. Paige flew across the small space that separated them and into Hawk's arms.

She feels so good in my arms.
I'm so glad he's here.
I wasn't sure I'd ever see her again.
I was afraid I'd never see him again.
Dear God, how I love this woman.
How can I hide my love for this man?

"You okay?" Hawk rasped past a tightened throat.

Her head was buried in his chest, but she nodded vigorously. "I'm fine, now that you're here."

He smiled, holding her close. "You know, all you would have had to do was tell me you were bored. We could have hiked out together."

She laughed, her voice shaking slightly. "Now why didn't I think of that? It *was* a rather lonely hike."

He let go of her reluctantly, then swung the heavy pack off his shoulders. "I brought you your bed. Thought it might be a little more comfortable."

"I haven't really been cold. The fire was nice."

"You did a good job of building it. I'm proud of you."

She tried to see his eyes in the flickering light from the fire. "Are you?"

He nodded. "More than you can possibly imagine."

"I'm glad."

A strong current flowed between them and their minds seemed to touch, to recall another place, another time, when their love and their need to express that love had almost overwhelmed them.

Hawk broke the tension between them by turning away. "Let me get the tent up and you can have the sleeping bag. I'll sleep by the fire." He became very busy as he continued to explain. "We can take off at daylight. It shouldn't be much farther to some sign of civilization." His matter-of-fact words were given away by the gruffness in his voice.

Paige silently helped to spread the canvas, the two of them working together in unspoken harmony. Within minutes a new camp was ready.

"Have you eaten?" she asked, breaking the silence at last. The unspoken communication was tearing at her emotions.

"I had some jerky and leftover sourdough bread," he admitted. "I didn't want to stop and heat up something."

"Do you want anything now?"

The multiple meaning hung in the air between them, daring him to give her an honest answer.

"No, I'll wait until morning. I need to get some rest." He sat down near her blanket and began to tug off his boots.

Paige watched him uncertainly. What did she expect from him? She realized that whatever she wanted, she would have to let him know. He was not the kind of man to take advantage of a situation, no matter what she'd accused him of earlier in the day.

What did she want? She crawled into the tent and found the sleeping bag open and waiting for her. She slid out of her shirt and slacks, glad to have the privacy of the tent and the freedom away from the constricting clothes. Then she stretched out in the bag and sighed. Its padding was heavenly after the hard surface she'd been lying on—that Hawk was now lying on. She sat up, wondering if he were already asleep.

She lifted the flap. He was stretched out on the blanket, his hands behind his head, staring at the fire. The movement from the tent caught his attention and he glanced over at her.

"You okay?"

She smiled. That was a familiar question with him. Was she okay? She wasn't sure. She wasn't sure about anything. All she knew was that she loved him and she wanted to be with him.

"Why don't you sleep in here?" she asked.

His slow smile disarmed her. "Don't tempt me. I'm afraid I'm fresh out of willpower this evening."

She swallowed, trying to dislodge the lump in her throat. "I'm inviting you to share the sleeping bag with me, Hawk. I'm not insisting your willpower accompany you."

Surprised, he stared at her across the intervening space. There was no way he could misinterpret her suggestion.

Like a sleepwalker Hawk came slowly to his feet. He leaned over and methodically picked up his boots and blanket, then padded softly over to her.

Paige scooted back from the door, giving him room to crawl in. The only light inside the tent was the reflection of the brightly burning fire through the canvas. She crawled inside the bag and waited.

For a moment, Hawk made no movement. Then he slowly began to undress. She heard the rustle of his clothes, and her heart kept up its steady thumping to the harsh sounds of his breathing. She felt him reach for the cover, and she raised it, guiding his hand inside. She heard his breath catch, and then he was lying beside her.

Never had the sleeping bag seemed so small. They had only been able to share it because she'd slept practically on top of him. It took only a moment for her to find the position she'd grown used to—her head on his shoulder, her body snuggled against him, her leg tucked between his. But the tension between them now was almost unbearable.

Hawk tried to control his breathing and his heartbeat. He tried to think of every unpleasant chore he'd ever had to do. He tried to forget the woman in his arms. Then she shifted, and he was lost.

"Hawk?" she whispered.

"Hmm?"

"Teach me how to love you." She felt the heavy thudding of his heart beneath the palm of her hand. Paige raised her head slightly until her lips rested softly against his.

Hawk tightened his arms around her and deepened the kiss. He had waited a lifetime for this woman, and for whatever reason she was now in his arms. He had tried to resist her, but could no longer fight what they both wanted to happen.

Paige had learned a great deal about making love that afternoon by the waterfall. For the first time she'd discovered her sensuous nature and learned something about Hawk's. She wanted to give him pleasure, to express her love for him in every way she could.

Paige was only a shadowy figure in the darkened tent, but Hawk's memory of the afternoon told him how she looked as she lay in his arms tenderly kissing him along his jawline. He could feel the slight perspiration on his forehead, caused by the restraints he'd placed on himself. He didn't want to hurt her by rushing their lovemaking, but his pent-up emotions were taking their toll.

Slowly he turned her over, then carefully lowered himself to her. Her arms snaked around his neck in an eager embrace, reassuring him of her lack of fear. Hawk slid his hands under her hips, carefully positioning her. Then his mouth found hers once more. This woman was his; he knew that in some deep, fundamental way. He found her waiting for him, and he took her with warm tenderness and loving patience.

Paige trembled with the force of her feelings. *I belong to him now,* she thought with a sense of rightness. She felt surrounded and consumed by him, swept up in the wonder of his possession—and in the tingling of desire that raced through her when he began the gentle rocking movement deep within her.

She held him closer, ever closer, learning to meet his rhythm, to join it, to experience the inexplicable joy of physical union between two people who have already merged their emotions.

She could feel the hard muscles of his back beneath her fingertips; his hands caressing her sides, then sliding to her breasts; his mouth as it memorized the contours of her face. Most of all, she could feel a tension inside of her, as though a spring was being wound, tighter and tighter, and she gasped as it suddenly seemed to project her straight up into the moonlit sky, a cascade of stars spreading its brilliance around her.

Hawk made one final lunge, then held her in a grip so tight she could scarcely breathe. He rolled over, still holding her, and gasped for air. Resting on his chest was like trying to float on a tidal wave, and Paige chuckled.

Hawk growled, "That is not a proper response to my lovemaking, I'll have you know. I think my heart is going to quit on me any minute, and all you can do is laugh!"

She stroked his jaw. "Not at you, love. Never at you. I was just thinking about what an active pillow I've found to rest my head on."

She could feel his grin against her palm. He shifted so that she could lie by his side and he sat up, reaching for his backpack.

"What are you doing?" she asked with relaxed interest.

"Getting a towel. I feel like I've been in the shower."

"You mean making love to me is like taking a shower?"

"Hardly." He relaxed back beside her, pulling her close. "Did I hurt you?"

"If you did, I wasn't aware of it." She leaned up to try to see his face, but it was too dark. "Hawk? Is it always like that?"

"I have no idea. It's never been like that for me before."

"I just wondered. Because if it was, I've got many years to regret. I had no idea making love could be so beautiful."

"Neither did I. You see, that's the first time I've ever made *love*." He sighed. "I may never recover."

Paige placed her head on his shoulder with a contented smile. If she had her way, he never would.

Nine

Paige's dream was delightful—full of light and color and happiness. She and Hawk were together, loving each other, on their honeymoon—honeymoon? Her eyes flew open, and it was as though her dream continued.

She was curled against Hawk's chest, her head resting against the soft movement of his breathing, her hand resting over his heart. Her body was tucked neatly by his side, her thigh intimately nestled between his. Overhead a bright sun beat down on the canvas so that she felt as though they were gingerbread people baking in an oven.

Hawk stirred beneath her, pulling her closer against him. There was a satisfying familiarity about the scene that Paige found reassuring. It was the slight differences that caused her heart to race.

This morning there were no clothes to separate them, and the slight soreness Paige experienced was new. Hawk's hold on her was much more possessive. His hand covered her breast as though for protection.

She glanced up at his face. He looked tired. She realized she'd never seen him asleep. In the past, he'd already been gone by the time she woke up. Now she studied him with a newfound possessiveness.

She studied the thick line of his brows that almost touched across his nose and noted the way his skin glistened in the warmth of the tent. Dark lashes rested against high cheekbones that gave him an autocratic, almost arrogant appearance. Her finger lightly touched his wide, strong chin, then traced the firm jawline to his ear.

He jerked his head suddenly and captured the tip of her finger between his teeth. She yelped.

"Is that any way to treat your tired old Indian guide when he's trying to catch up on his sleep?" he complained in a husky voice.

She leaned over him, watching him with suspicion. His eyes remained closed. "Why is it my fault you're tired?" she asked with interest.

His hand slid around the back of her neck and coaxed her mouth to within a couple of inches of his. "Honey, if you can't remember that, you've got a bigger problem with your memory than we guessed." His mouth captured hers in a lazy kiss that effectively ended their teasing.

Of course she remembered. She remembered waking up during the night to Hawk's erotic touch as he gave a strong impression of a man determined to memorize every inch of her body. How could she forget?

His lovemaking had been slow and very thorough. She felt that she could spend the rest of her life in his arms and never grow bored.

"Shouldn't we be leaving?" she managed to whisper when his kiss finally ended.

"We should have left several hours ago," he admitted ruefully.

She started to shift her leg and his thighs clamped down on her like a vise, effectively holding her prisoner—a very willing prisoner. From that position she could tell the effect she had on him. Even as inexperienced as she was, she'd had the ability to respond to him, to satisfy him—and to keep him still wanting her. Paige sighed with fervent pleasure.

He pulled her over on top of him. She grinned. "Is this what is considered the view from the top?"

"Could be. What do you think?"

"I think I could become addictive."

His mouth found the soft spot at the base of her neck where her pulse quivered. His tongue explored the area until she shivered, then he pressed his lips along a trail to her chin, tipping her head down until he found her mouth.

Time no longer mattered. They were lost in the pleasure of learning more about each other. Hawk introduced her to new sensations, new intimacies, that carried Paige to a dimension where she could share the intense love she felt for Hawk by expressing it in arousing and exhilarating ways.

This morning Paige set the rhythm for their lovemaking. From her position on top of Hawk she discovered how to tease and torment him until his greater strength finally forced her to accept his hard length within her, a most satisfactory conclusion for both of them to her teasing. She slowly built the spiraling emotional structure that led them to the top, where they soared together on a mindless plane of sensation and pleasure, slowly circling back to earth, wrapped in each other's arms. Then, limp from her exertions, Paige lay quietly on Hawk's chest, content to rest.

Because her ear was pressed against his chest, she heard the rumble of his voice as the words left his lips. "We need to be moving, love."

She raised her head and stared at him in bewilderment. "I thought we were."

His smile lit up the small tent. "I mean we need to get down the trail...what there is of it, anyway."

"Oh." She dropped her head and thought about her father. She and Hawk had been together for almost a week. That meant he'd had his heart attack seven days ago. Seven days. If he'd survived the initial attack, he would have passed the crisis stage by now. Had he made it?

She sat up, sliding off Hawk in one graceful movement. He pretended overwhelming relief that he could now breathe again, but she ignored him. She also ignored her lack of clothing when she threw the flap of the tent open and stepped out of the tent. It was another beautiful day.

She glanced down at her shoulder and discovered a long scratch, no doubt picked up on her travels the day before. Walking over to the edge of the swollen stream, she knelt down to wash off the scratch and rinse her face.

Paige only had a moment's warning before hands grasped her around the waist and she was propelled into the river, securely held against a large, warm body.

They hit the water with a resounding splash. Her squeal of shock was due as much to the unexpected push as it was to the temperature of the water. She came up sputtering, discovering she was little more than waist-deep in the clear running river. Hawk was sitting so that the water came almost to his neck.

"That was rude!" she declared in her most haughty, well-bred tones.

"Was it?" His look of repentance needed a little work to be convincing.

"I could have drowned."

"Not while I was holding you."

His infectious grin totally destroyed her efforts to solemnly discuss the deficiencies of his deportment as reflected by his recent behavior. She resolved the matter by splashing water in his face and an olympic-sized water fight ensued, scaring the wildlife around their campsite.

Paige couldn't remember when she'd ever acted so childish—certainly not as a child nor as an earnest adolescent. When they discovered, to no one's surprise, that Hawk could outmaneuver, outswim and outguess Paige, she conceded defeat and proceeded to bathe herself, as though getting into the water had been entirely her own idea.

By the time she crawled out of the river to dry her hair in the sun, Hawk had their meal prepared. Paige was surprised to discover how unself-conscious she was with him. She grabbed his shirt to put on after drying herself, and ate unconcernedly, oblivious to the side glances she received from Hawk. She was modestly covered. It wasn't her fault that he was aware of what she didn't have on underneath that shirt.

"I never thought I'd ever be envious of a piece of my clothing," he said after finishing his cup of coffee. He stood up, staring down at the cleavage revealed by the loose shirt.

In the carefully modulated tone of a professional doctor, she inquired, "Tell me, sir, how long have you noticed having this insatiable sexual appetite?"

He leaned over and picked up her empty dishes and shrugged. "Only since being around you, doctor."

"I see. Then the cure is obvious." She stood up and headed toward the tent.

"Is it?" His gaze followed her graceful body as she walked away from him.

She stopped and looked back over her shoulder. "Of course. Remove the source, and you remove the problem." She disappeared inside the tent.

He washed up their dishes and deftly packed them away. "Isn't that a rather drastic solution?" He raised his voice so that she would hear him.

A few minutes later she stepped out, chastely covered in her own rather bedraggled clothes, a little worse for the wear they'd had the day before. "Drastic, perhaps, but certainly effective."

They pulled the tent down in companionable silence. When he had everything back in his knapsack, giving Paige a smaller pack to carry, Hawk finally admitted, "I'd prefer a less effective cure, if you could arrange it."

Following the river, Hawk started off and Paige fell in step behind him. She admired the width of his shoulders and the seemingly weightless way he carried the pack that she knew must weigh at least sixty pounds. "Well, it might take some experimenting, trying various concepts, to find a suitable cure."

Without turning around, he answered, "Whatever you say, doc. I know I'm in good hands, so you have my permission to experiment to your heart's content."

My heart will be content only when you're around, she decided, but thought it more politic not to mention it.

Hawk set a steady pace that seemed to eat up the miles. He was an expert at picking the easiest path, Paige discovered, and wished she'd managed to control her feelings enough not to have struck out on her own the day before.

When the way was rough, Hawk helped her, and Paige discovered her most exhilarating feeling came with his silent look of admiration when she determinedly stayed up with him.

It was midafternoon when their good luck seemed to run out. The river disappeared underground through a hole in the canyon wall.

Hawk stood there, his hands on his hips, and studied the rugged terrain around them. They were in some type of canyon and there didn't seem to be a way out. "Why don't we stop here? It's a good place to eat and get some rest," he finally said.

Paige sank down gratefully. Her body had been protesting the unusual treatment for the past two hours, but she'd been determined not to ask Hawk to stop. They were hiking out because she'd insisted. She refused to admit it was too much for her.

Hawk was right. There was shade here, and the water was still sparkling clear. With some stiffness Paige knelt by the river and scooped it up in her hands to drink. Then she splashed it on her face to cool off. Was it only that morning that they had played in the water? It seemed years ago.

Their entire time together seemed to have lasted forever. She could scarcely remember her life before Hawk and she refused to think about what it would be like when they returned to their daily routines. All she had was here and now. It was enough, because it had to be enough.

Hawk handed her a large piece of sourdough bread and a piece of jerky. A cup of cold water was in his other hand.

"Thank you," she murmured, seating herself cross-legged under a shade tree a short distance away.

Hawk stared at her, concerned. Had he pushed her too hard? She sounded different—as though they were barely acquainted, as though they knew nothing about each other, or as though she cared nothing for him.

That was the difference. From the time she was aware of him after their forced landing, she had been warm to him. Wary, perhaps, but she'd projected a strong vibration of caring. Now it was almost as though she'd erected a shield between them. He wondered if it were to protect herself or him. He sat down next to her, biting into the bread and staring into the distance.

Perhaps she was trying to protect him. She'd had time to come to terms with their new relationship, or rather, their lack of a formal one. Yet she had given herself to him—totally, without reservation. What did it mean?

Had she finally found a man who could arouse her and she'd decided to further her education? What did he mean to her? What could he mean? She was a career woman—he was a maverick.

Hawk finished eating, then stretched out in the shade and closed his eyes. He refused to worry about it. He had nothing to offer her and they both knew it. He'd learned at an early age to take what life offered and not question it. As a philosophy, it wasn't a bad way to survive. The secret was not to want something you could never have.

Paige studied Hawk's relaxed position and envied him his ability to fall asleep immediately, to wake up alert, and to be in control of his emotions at all times. Her problem was that he had stirred up emotions within her she'd never known existed. Now that they were alive and well and clamoring to be used, she didn't know what to do with them.

Trying to deal with emotions on an intellectual basis was impossible. Emotions were like errant children, bounding out of control at the least provocation. No matter how much time she spent reasoning with them, they proceeded to go their merry way, ignoring the consequences.

What she had to keep in mind was the importance of getting to Flagstaff. Up until now, her father and her profession had been her entire life. She could only pray that her father was all right.

She mentally listed all the positive items in his favor—his relative youth, the fact that he did take care of himself, and that he knew the importance of good health. Paige had to leave him in God's hands, but she prayed that God in his mercy would grant her a few more years with him.

For the first time in her life, Paige faced how much she'd taken her father for granted. Although she'd loved her mother, her thinking processes had been more like her father's and she'd had trouble relating to her maternal parent. She understood her mother's pain at being on the outskirts of her father's life, but

she couldn't relate to it, because she had made herself
a part of his life as soon as she could.

*Instead of sitting around wishing for something,
I've always gone after what I wanted,* she realized in
surprise. The sudden insight into her own character
surprised her. Paige had never been one to spend much
time in self-analysis.

"We need to go, Paige..." Hawk's deep voice
brought her out of a surprisingly deep sleep. She
hadn't meant to sleep, only to rest her eyes. Hawk
stood over her with one hand outstretched. She
grasped it and pulled herself up. He increased her
momentum so that she fell against him. With calm
deliberation he found her mouth with his and gave her
a leisurely, but very thorough, kiss.

Damn him! Her new resolution to hold herself aloof
from him disappeared, and she could feel her body
melt against him. *It just isn't fair.* She returned his kiss
with fervor, until he pulled away from her, his expression strained.

"I'd like to get out of this area before nightfall.
Hopefully it levels out down a little lower. There's a
possibility the river will return to the surface and we
can find it."

Once again Hawk led the way, and Paige followed.
She couldn't help but wonder what would have happened to them if she'd had another kind of pilot, one
who didn't know how to survive in the wilderness. She
shook her head impatiently. *Don't think about it. Just
be thankful for Hawk.*

She had reason to reiterate that thought several
times as the rugged miles continued to unroll beneath
their feet. The river no longer guided them. They

scrambled up one side of a hill, then down the other. Paige wondered how Hawk knew which way to go. She was turned around in her directions. She was also exhausted.

Twilight was beginning to place its mystical touch around them when Hawk finally halted. "We'll camp here."

Paige wearily looked around. The place looked no different than many other places they'd passed, but she asked no questions at all. Instead she helped Hawk put up the tent, spread the sleeping bag, gather wood and prepare a simple meal.

They were both too tired for conversation. They spent little time in front of the fire after eating. Instead they both stripped down and crawled into the sleeping bag, immediately falling asleep.

It was light outside, but the sun wasn't up when Hawk gently shook Paige awake. She groaned, trying to find her comforting pillow. "We need to get started, love," he said in a low voice that brought her out of her dream-filled sleep.

Paige sat up groggily, feeling aches and pains in places she'd never known existed. She'd thought she was in good physical condition, but this little outing was rapidly convincing her otherwise.

Hawk felt as though a hand was tightening around his heart as he watched her painful movements. He'd been amazed at her stamina and the valiant effort she'd been making. But they couldn't afford to waste time now. They were away from water, and their food supply was dwindling. He had to do everything he could to find a settlement of some sort that day.

Paige reluctantly pulled on her clothes, vowing to burn them as soon as she found a place to buy more.

She was sick of them, sick of walking, sick of trying to keep up with the robot she was with who never seemed to get tired, or hungry, or thirsty. She glared up at him and froze. The tender look in his eyes caused tears to form in her eyes.

She slipped her arms around his neck. "Oh, Hawk, I love you so much. I'm sorry to be such a tenderfoot."

His arms came around her in a fierce hug. "I love you, too. And you're doing fine, just fine. We should be out of here today."

She pulled back from him in surprise. "You think so?"

He nodded, unwilling to make a more emphatic statement on such an uncertainty.

She hugged him back. "Won't that be great? Just think how it will feel to have a hot bath for a change, and eat something besides jerky and dried fruit, and sleep in a nice, comfortable bed, and ..."

"But madam, you paid an incredible amount of money for this special safari into the wilds of eastern Arizona. I thought you wanted to get your money's worth." His fake British accent was very well done.

"That's true, young man, very true. However, you didn't mention the exercise program in your brochure, or I might have had second thoughts."

He scratched his head thoughtfully. "Perhaps we should revise the brochure, do you think?"

"Definitely. But don't expect an overwhelming amount of people to sign up."

He drew himself up to his full height. "But madam, we only cater to the most elite clientele. Surely you recognized that."

She looked at their clothes, white with dust, ragged and torn, and at the battered camping supplies that had kept them going, and she laughed. "I'm glad to hear it. I want nothing but the best. I thought that was understood." Her gaze turned back to him. "I'm so glad I got it."

She was irresistible in that mood, and he didn't even try to resist. Instead he gathered her into his arms and kissed her with all the fervency he possessed.

A few minutes later he let her down with a sigh. "We still need to leave."

"I know."

"I could stay here all day and make love to you, you know that, don't you?"

"I'm glad," she whispered, in awe of the miracle that had brought them together and caused such similar strong feelings to occur in each of them for the other.

Hawk firmly set her aside and left the tent, and Paige hurriedly repacked what they had taken out of the backpack the night before, then efficiently rolled up the sleeping bag. She was getting almost as good at packing as Hawk. Almost.

A little hero worship never hurt anyone, she decided. Wearily she crawled out of the tent to begin a new day.

Ten

The river reappeared about midmorning but was nothing like the one they'd been following. This one seemed out of control, raging along in a rolling frenzy.

Hawk found a small pocket of shallow water that had already been heated by the sun and suggested they take time to bathe. Paige hadn't realized what a luxury water could be. It felt so good to feel clean again. She took her hair down and washed it, luxuriating in the cool water.

It's amazing how different your outlook is when you're clean and well fed, Paige decided, looking for Hawk to share her bit of philosophy. But when she spotted him, all previous thoughts flew from her head. He stood under a rocky overhang where part of the river gushed over the side, taking a vigorous shower.

She could only stare at his unconscious male beauty. His bronzed skin glistened in the sunlight and water, and she visually traced a path from his broad chest to his waist and hips, down to his thighs and well-developed calves. Only his feet were hidden in the swirling water.

Paige slicked her wet hair back from her face, then started swimming toward him, ignoring the pull of the current. The bubbling water broke over her head several times, but her gaze never left the man ahead of her.

Hawk had turned his back to her, his face raised to the hard-driving water, and didn't hear her approach. She waded out of the deeper water until he was close enough to touch. He couldn't have heard her with the rushing water all around him; he could only have sensed her presence. But he turned as though knowing she were there.

The message in her eyes was unmistakable, and it fanned a flame within him that had never gone out since the first time he saw her.

Without a word he scooped her up in his arms and strode out of the water. Their things were packed, but he spotted the blanket she had made into a small pack for her, and without breaking stride he reached for it, shook it out and lowered her on one side of it. She watched as he flicked the other half open.

Still without speaking, Hawk reached for her, his need obvious. Their communication was more basic than words, and when she flowed into his arms an explosion of desire swept over them.

There was no gentleness between them. Instead theirs was a fierce enactment of possession. They belonged together—they belonged to each other—and they used the act of love to reinforce that statement. Hawk took her in a powerful, surging drive and she was with him all the way. Her arms locked around his neck and her legs wrapped around him, encouraging the savage swirl of emotions that gripped them.

You're mine, you're mine, you belong to me, only to me—his rhythm matched the litany of phrases running through his head. She responded to him as though she had heard the refrain and affirmed it.

Paige found herself once again in that other world of pleasurable sensation, her body flexing convulsively as she toppled over the edge of the sky. Hawk's harsh breathing filled her world when he made his final plunge, then collapsed in her arms, his chest heaving.

I feel that every part of me has melted and remolded itself around him. She enjoyed the weight of his body pressing against her; knew that he'd lost control this time, and she was reassured. He hadn't been able to completely hide from her what he was feeling.

They lay there, bodies intertwined, as the world began to impinge once more on their consciousness. Hawk shifted, rolling free of her and sat up. His folded arms rested against his raised knees and his head dropped against his arms.

"I'm sorry."

Paige felt too limp to move, but she forced herself into a sitting position. "For what?"

"For being so rough."

"It's obvious I'm beyond redemption, then. I enjoyed it. Thoroughly."

He raised his head and stared at her smiling face. Then he rested his forehead against hers. "Oh, Paige, you're a constant surprise. You never say what I expect. You're not like anyone I've ever known." He sighed. "What am I going to do with you?"

She tried to sound light and cheerful. "Love me?"

His black eyes glistened with emotion. "Is that enough?"

She stared at him, feeling his uncertainty as though it were her own. And perhaps it was. "It will have to be."

Midafternoon found them facing a dilemma. They needed to cross the river, but the rushing water had widened to a dangerous degree. There were no fordable spots that Hawk could find.

He toyed with the alternative. They could stay on this side of the river in the hope it would continue toward civilization. But crossing was the quickest way to get to help. He had spotted their first sign of the twentieth century over the last rise—a towering antenna standing tall on the next ridge over from them. That antenna had to have a power station nearby, which meant there was a road to follow. It was time to leave their guide, the river. But first they had to cross it.

Hawk planned carefully. He made them stop and eat first. Then he built a small raft to carry their provisions. They stripped down to essentials, so that the heavy drag of water wouldn't catch in their clothes. He was thankful the bedroll and tent were in waterproof containers.

The care he took in making the crossing would have placed them safely on the other side, except for one unforeseen detail, and that detail made a mockery of all his precautions.

They laughed when all of their provisions and clothes were neatly strapped to the small raft. "Do you realize that if we lose that raft, we'll never dare come out of hiding?" Paige stood there in her brief shorts and blouse tied under her breasts. Hawk had dispensed with everything but his briefs.

"Now's a lousy time to ask, but how good of a swimmer are you?" he asked with a slight smile. The smile didn't reach his concerned eyes.

"Better than average," she assured him. "I haven't won any gold medals or anything, but I can stay afloat."

He glanced over at the water that was moving swiftly past. "It's hard to tell how deep it is along here, but there's no way to cross either upstream or downstream from here, so this place wins by default." A limb came floating by, then disappeared in the suction of the water. "The rains up in the mountains must have caused this heavy flow. Normally by July the mountain streams are quiet and subdued."

"I guess somebody forgot to point out the date to this one."

"A definite oversight, but it can't be helped." He stepped off the bank into water up to his knees. Dragging the small raft alongside him, he motioned to her. "I'm not going to hang on to you. It would be more of a hindrance than a help." He pointed to the other bank about 150 yards downstream. "That's where we'll end up, hopefully. When the current catches you, keep swimming as straight as you can." He watched as she slid into the water beside him.

Just one more adventure to tell my grandkids, she decided with characteristic resolution.

Hawk gave her a head start, wanting to keep her in his line of vision. He pulled the raft along beside him, keeping it upstream of him so that he would have better control—which is why he didn't see the tree stump suddenly churn up to the surface right beside him.

He didn't have time to evade it. The long roots caught the raft, flipping it high into the air, and the tree trunk slammed into Hawk, carrying him down the river in its curling grasp.

Paige was concentrating on putting as much power into each stroke as she had. She was wondering how long she could keep it up when she heard a loud, crashing sound behind her. She jerked her head around in time to see the raft go tumbling and Hawk disappear beneath the tree stump.

"Hawk!"

Water sloshed into her mouth and she sputtered. She fought to keep her head out of the water and began to swim furiously after the twisting, turning stump. The swirling water kept washing over her, and she couldn't keep up with the stump.

She had to find Hawk. He had to be all right. She closed her eyes for a split second, frightened at the thought that he might not be all right. Not Hawk. He was too strong. He'd been through too many things and survived. He was tough. He'd make it. She knew he'd make it.

At first she thought her foot had caught on something in the river. Then she realized she'd found bottom. With her last remaining strength Paige pulled herself through the dragging water until she reached dry land and collapsed in a heap. She lay there, gasping for air, praying for strength. She had to get up and find Hawk—he needed her.

When Paige opened her eyes she knew too much time had passed. The sun had moved into the west. Shaking, she got to her feet and looked around. The ridge where the antenna stood was no longer visible. She wasn't even sure which direction to look. She only knew it was somewhere on this side of the river.

The river continued to rush by, but there was no sign of Hawk. She felt a burning and looked down at her legs, absently noting they were raw with scrapes. She ignored them.

Hawk had gone downstream. Therefore, she had to go downstream. It was a fundamental decision, one that took no effort at all. She couldn't afford to waste her energy—she had to find Hawk.

Paige stumbled along the river, but saw no sign of anyone. It was as though she were completely alone in this strange world. *Maybe Hawk found the tree stump provided faster transportation.* She forced her shoulders straight and continued walking.

It was only when she spotted their raft, innocently floating along the edge of the river, that she cried. She cried all the while she tugged it from the water and spread their clothes and provisions out to dry. She wasn't even sure why. So much had gotten wet, maybe that was it. Or maybe it was because Hawk had taken so much care to protect her and their belongings, but had not taken enough care of himself.

I'm not going to let you leave me, damn you, or our things. I'll find you, if it takes all night.

It didn't take all night.

The sun had set, casting its last scarlet rays into the sky, when Paige saw something lying in the water. She couldn't run; the pack she carried weighted her so that she was forced to place each foot carefully in order to keep her balance. She wasn't even sure she wanted to find out what it was.

Hawk was draped over a large rock protruding near the center of the river. When the stump sweeping him along downstream had connected with the rock, the stump had catapulted into the air, freeing him. But by that time he was barely conscious.

He'd hung on to the rock until he found the strength to crawl up on it, but didn't have the strength to make it to shore.

Paige dropped the pack and stared at him. He looked so pale and still, but he was breathing. One side of his face was bloodied and bruised, but he was alive. His side looked as though he'd been kicked by an angry bull.

If she could just get to him.

Then she remembered the raft. How far back was it? She couldn't remember, but it didn't matter. She had to find it. Paige dropped the backpack and hurried back along the way she'd come, fear lending speed to her failing body.

The light was rapidly fading by the time she returned. Hawk hadn't moved.

They would need a fire, but she didn't want to take the time to build one until she could get him to dry land. At least the large rock he had found was big enough to take his full length, so he hadn't been subjected to the continual pounding of the water.

She slipped into the water, surprised at how much colder it felt, and pushed the raft ahead of her. The current wasn't too bad on this side of the large rock, and she only had to go a small distance where her feet wouldn't touch bottom.

"Hawk?" she pulled herself up beside him, struggling not to lose her grip on the raft. "Hawk, please answer me." She dipped her hand in the water, then brushed it across his face.

He groaned.

"We need to get you out of here, Hawk. Can you help me?"

His eyelids fluttered, then were still. She didn't have time to waste. By gently shoving on his unhurt side she managed to shift him until he began to slide into the water. Paige quickly grabbed the raft and maneuvered it under his head. If she could just keep them afloat, they would make it.

Paige never remembered the details of that nightmare journey back to shore, or how she managed to get him out of the water. But she did it. She rolled him onto the blanket and then dragged him next to the fire she managed to build. Once again Hawk's precautions had helped—the matches had stayed dry in their waterproof pouch.

Her next priority was to examine his wounds. From the flickering light of the campfire she could see that one side of his face was bruised, swollen and scratched, although most of the bleeding had stopped. His side was scraped raw from his armpit to his hip.

His pulse was strong and steady—a reassuring sign—but he had an angry welt across his forehead, which could explain his unconscious state. *This seems to be our trip for head wounds. I wonder if you'll know who I am when you wake up.*

She needed to get him warm. She warmed the blanket by the fire, making sure it was dry before wrapping him up in it once more.

When his eyes opened, she could have wept with relief. Instead she stroked his cheek and asked, "How do you feel?"

He stared up at her, his eyes dulled with pain. Then they seemed to focus on her face and brighten. "I'm not sure," he whispered. "Kinda like I've been in a barroom brawl." He touched the side of his face and winced.

"As a matter of fact—" she tried to keep her voice steady and unconcerned "—that's what you look like." She brushed his hair back. "How does your side feel?"

Hawk drew a breath, then abruptly stopped, pain obvious on his face. "Like hell."

"I can't be certain without X rays, but you may have a cracked rib or two. You took quite a jolt."

"What happened?"

"What do you remember?"

A gleam appeared in his eyes that could have been amusement at their reversed positions. "I remember swimming across the river and something hitting me. What was it?"

"A tree stump. You got caught in the roots and were dragged downstream."

He lay there, staring at her. "I could have drowned."

"Yes."

"How did you find me?"

She forced a smile. "Easy. You were sunning yourself on a rock in the middle of the river when I came along."

He frowned. "I remember that—I remember trying to hang on so I wouldn't be swept back into the water."

"You did a great job of hanging on. When I found you, you'd crawled up on top of it."

He looked at her, disbelief plain on his face. "You found me on the rock?"

"Uh-huh."

"How the hell did you get me off it?"

"I used the raft. You should be pleased with your construction skills. It took quite a beating today, but it's still intact."

She placed her hand on his forehead. He felt warm. Too warm.

Paige nonchalantly came to her feet. "I think I'll put the tent up now. I'm very glad to report the waterproof cover kept the sleeping bag from getting soaked. You could write all kinds of endorsements for your camping gear after this trip."

Hawk tried to respond with a smile, but the pain and swelling in his jaw stopped him. Paige tucked the blanket tighter around him, then left his side. Within moments he was asleep.

The tent was much tougher to put up by herself, but Paige managed. The sleeping bag was warm from being spread in front of the fire by the time she arranged it inside the tent.

Hawk was still asleep when she returned to his side. "Hawk? Can you walk to the tent? Your bed is ready."

He roused himself, staring around the area as though trying to get his bearings. With Paige's help he made it to bed, then dutifully drank the hot soup she brought him.

Paige could see his pain, and fear clutched at her. He wasn't going to be able to go any farther—not on his own.

What were they going to do?

Afraid that she would hurt him if she shared the sleeping bag with him, Paige wrapped up in the blanket and stretched out by his side. Never had she felt so helpless to care for someone.

She checked on him several times during the night. He was restless and feverish, but never awakened. Paige made sure he stayed covered, fearing complications due to exposure. It was almost dawn when she dozed off, and later she thought she was dreaming because she heard voices. They were speaking in a language she didn't recognize. Paige woke up with a start, realizing that someone was outside.

She jerked open the flap and crawled out of the tent. Two men stood there, staring at her as though a Martian had landed in front of them demanding to find their leader. She felt the same way. They were dressed in Levi's and plaid Western shirts, but their hair was long and tied at the nape of their necks. Their Western hats shaded bronzed faces. Unsmiling bronzed faces.

"Did you know you're on posted property here, lady?" one of them finally asked.

She burst out laughing, almost hysterical with relief. "Are we? Well, you see, we really aren't camping, even though it looks like it. Our plane was forced down up there... She waved her arm over her shoulder and they looked up at the mountain range behind her, then back at her with twin expressions of disbelief. "My...uh, friend was hurt yesterday when we crossed the river. Is there any way we can get him to a doctor?"

She knew better than to explain that she was a doctor. She could tell she'd stretched her credibility with them to the outer limits.

One of them stepped inside of the tent. When he came out he spoke to his companion, but not in English. His friend nodded and disappeared through the trees.

"Where's he going?" she asked in alarm. Didn't they care that Hawk was hurt?

The remaining man answered, "He's gone to bring a truck up here. It's too far to carry him."

"Oh."

"He's Apache, isn't he?"

Surprised, she said, "I believe so. Why do you ask?"

The man grinned, changing his austere expression into a friendly one. "Are you aware you're on the Apache Reservation?"

She shook her head.

"I don't recognize him. Is he from around here?"

"He said he's originally from Dulce, New Mexico."

"Ahhh. A Jicarilla." He nodded, seemingly satisfied.

Paige looked around. "How long will it take your friend to get here?"

"He should make it in about an hour."

She went over to their supplies and found the coffeepot. "I thought I'd make some coffee, then try to get Hawk to drink some water."

"Your friend's name is Hawk?"

"That's right."

"You don't hear those names much anymore. My name is John Anthony. My friend is Roger Thomas."

"Oh." Why did she feel as though she'd stumbled into an Alice in Wonderland scene?

They'd made it. They'd found their way out of the wilderness and down to civilization. She glanced at the man hunched over, feeding the fire. Yes. Civilization. *Oh, Hawk, if you could only enjoy this with me. We made it, thanks to you. Please get well for me.*

Paige sat back from the bed, pleased to see Hawk resting naturally. They'd been brought to a mobile home by their rescuers, who'd explained they were almost a day's drive from the closest town. They'd put Hawk to bed and she'd begun to bathe him with cold water, trying to get his temperature down.

His fever had finally broken. She'd been afraid of pneumonia, but she was beginning to hope the worst was over. After two days of vigil by his bedside, Paige felt limp with exhaustion.

Deciding that it was safe to leave him, she walked down the short hall to the kitchen. A young woman was stirring something that smelled delicious in a large pot. She smiled when Paige paused in the doorway.

"Hi. I'm sorry I wasn't here when you and your husband first arrived. I'm Alicia, John Anthony's daughter."

She was the picture of youthful freshness, Paige thought with a smile. Her tight faded jeans emphasized the shapely length of her legs in knee-high leather boots. A red T-shirt enhanced her dark skin, and her short haircut accented her large black eyes. A real beauty. She looked to be in her late teens.

First things first. "He isn't my husband. My name is Paige Winston. Hawk Cameron was flying me to

Flagstaff last week when we had to make an emergency landing.''

"Oh." Alicia's eyes lit up. "I went back to introduce myself when I got home, but you'd fallen asleep in the chair. Hawk looks like he's been in a fight."

"He was. With a tree stump. If you think *he* looks bad, you oughta see the other guy," she said with an exaggerated drawl.

They both laughed. Alicia's eyes sparkled. "He's very handsome, isn't he?" she asked shyly.

Paige could feel her reaction to Alicia's innocent words somewhere deep inside. "Yes, he is."

"Have you known him long?"

"No. Just since our mishap."

"So you don't know if he's married."

"I think it's a safe bet to guess he isn't."

Alicia's smile became even brighter. "Well, if there's anything I can do to help, please let me know."

"As a matter of fact, there is. Your father told me you didn't have a phone. Can you tell me where I might find one?"

Alicia thought for a moment. "The nearest one is about twenty-five miles from here." She grinned. "Twenty-five long miles—it takes hours to get there. I'm sure my father would be willing to give you a ride, though."

Paige sat down at the small kitchen table. Her brain seemed to be as sluggish as molasses.

Alicia dished up a steaming bowl of stew. "Here, have something to eat. After that why don't you take a nice, relaxing shower and get some sleep." She sat down across from Paige and looked at her with concern. "You look exhausted. If Hawk needs anything, I can either take care of him or call you." She reached over and softly patted Paige's hand. "You can sleep in my room if you'd like."

Paige could feel tears prickling at the back of her eyes and knew she'd been pushing herself too hard if a young girl's thoughtfulness could make her feel weepy.

"Thank you, Alicia. You and your dad have been great, taking us in like this."

Alicia's smile lit up the kitchen. "We've enjoyed having you. I'm just sorry we can't help out with a phone—your families must be frantic for some sort of word. You both were tremendously lucky."

"I know. Hawk made most of our luck. I wouldn't have made it without him."

Alicia's smile was very understanding. "He's really special, isn't he?"

"Yes," Paige murmured, "he really is."

When Hawk woke up the next morning he was surprised to see a young Indian girl sitting by his bed.

"Good morning," she offered shyly.

He tried to smile, but one side of his face felt like it was made of plaster of Paris. He felt along his cheekbone and discovered bandages covered half his face.

"Where am I?" He heard himself and almost groaned aloud. Not the most original question, but dammit, he seemed to have misplaced a few things— like a river, a raft and a companion. Before she could answer, he interrupted with, "Where's Paige?"

"Oh, she's asleep. She sat up with you until quite late last night. I told her I'd check on you if she wanted to go on to bed."

He mentally digested that, feeling better to know that Paige wasn't far away.

"This is my father's home," the young girl explained. "I'm Alicia Anthony. My father and a friend found you and Dr. Winston camping near the river day before yesterday, so they brought you here." She gave him a very sympathetic smile. "Dr. Winston said you were running a temperature."

He took a few minutes to consider the information Alicia gave him. So they'd been here for two days. He only had vague memories of warm hands caring for him and a soft voice. Paige. He smiled. It had been her turn to look after an invalid.

Hawk felt a tightness on his forehead and touched it lightly. A large bump sat above his right eye. "I must have really gotten a blow to my head to make a knot that big." He looked at the young girl who was watching him so intently. "I'm pretty hardheaded."

"Dr. Winston was quite concerned," she admitted. "You were very lucky to have a doctor with you."

"You know, I never thought of it that way. I guess you're right." He grinned, a lopsided grin to ease the tightness of his swollen jaw and face.

Alicia stared at him for a moment, her gaze admiring. Then, blushing, she rushed into speech to cover her confusion. "Dr. Winston was also trying to find out how she could get to Flagstaff. She seems most anxious to leave."

Of course. He'd forgotten about her father. They needed to leave right away.

"She explained that you were her pilot and she didn't want to leave you until she was sure you were going to be all right."

Her pilot. She doesn't want to leave...until I'm all right. He stared at the young girl. *Of course. Now*

we're in the real world and we revert back to our for-
mer roles. She's Dr. Winston and I'm just the pilot.

Hawk tried to sit up, and a pain shot through his
chest.

"Oh, Hawk, you shouldn't be moving around. Dr.
Winston said she's almost certain a couple of your ribs
are broken." She leaned over and pulled his pillow
higher. "Why don't you lie back and I'll bring you
something to eat? I bet you're starved!"

He glanced up into her glowing eyes, full of admiration. He ignored the pain in his side, and in his head.
He ignored the pain of knowing that whatever he and
Paige had shared was over. That was yesterday. He
had to live with today. He smiled at the girl hovering
anxiously beside him. "That sounds fine, just fine."

He would deal with his pain later, as he always did—
alone.

Eleven

The sound of Alicia's light, tinkling laugh settled like a feather in Paige's sleep, tickling at her consciousness, taunting her with its subtle sensuality.

When Paige had finally fallen asleep, she had succumbed to the deep, healing rest of the exhausted. Hawk's fever was down; she'd managed to tape up his ribs and to clean up the contusions and abrasions on his face and head. He was going to be all right.

She'd left him sleeping peacefully, but from the sounds in the other room he was not only awake but enjoying company. She heard the deep rumble of his voice, then Alicia's clear, delighted laughter.

Paige tried to ignore the twinge of pain that shot through her. He wasn't her personal property, after all. There hadn't even been the most rudimentary of commitments made. *Hadn't there?* she asked herself. *Perhaps not on his part, but you know very well you would never give yourself to a man if you hadn't made a commitment of love to him.*

She dug through her small supply of clothes and decided to try one of the skirts and blouses. They were sadly wrinkled but she took them into the small bathroom with her and hung them while she showered, hoping the wrinkles would disappear in the steam.

Has he asked for your commitment? Has he asked anything of you? Her inner voice continued to probe. She reviewed their time together, all of their conversations, and his lovemaking. He'd convinced her he'd never before experienced the feelings he'd shared with her. *That was something, wasn't it?* Perhaps, but what? Where did she stand with him now? Where did they go from here?

Paige had never before been faced with her own vulnerability, and she was afraid of what the future might bring.

After her shower, Paige dressed and did her hair carefully in the topknot she generally wore in the summer. Feeling much more like her old self, she went down the hall to see Hawk.

She found him sitting up in bed sipping a cup of coffee. A tray of empty dishes on the table nearby attested to the fact he had eaten, and well.

Alicia was seated by the bed, but hopped up when Paige walked in. "Your patient is doing much better this morning, doctor," she announced brightly.

Paige smiled at Hawk. "I'm certainly glad to hear it."

He did not return her smile. In fact, his glance was one he might have given a casual acquaintance. "I'm surprised to still find you here, Dr. Winston. I figured you'd be on your way to Flagstaff by now."

Dr. Winston? Then Paige glanced at Alicia's interested expression. *He wants to keep up appearances,
does he? I wonder why?*

Suddenly shy, Paige walked over to the side of the
bed and reached for his forehead. "Any fever this
morning?"

He flinched away from her hand. "Of course not.
There's nothing wrong with me but a few scrapes and
bruises." His voice was brusque.

"And a couple of broken ribs," she added.

"You don't know that for sure," he insisted.

"True. Without X rays, I can't be positive. But
there's every indication."

He shrugged, then winced. "Maybe so. But they'll
heal."

She grinned. "And you're tough, right?"

He stared at her, his expression giving nothing of his
thoughts away. "Tough enough."

Tension grew in the room, and even Alicia became
aware of it. She picked up the tray and said, "Well, I'll
go wash these up." She paused at the door and gave
Hawk a dazzling smile. "You behave now."

For the first time since Paige had walked into the
room Hawk's face relaxed into a soul-wrenching
smile. "I don't have the strength to do anything else."
His smile widened to a grin when she laughed.

"Why aren't you gone?" Hawk asked Paige in a
careless tone after Alicia disappeared down the hall.

"Because I didn't want to go off and leave you,"
she explained patiently.

He shifted restlessly in the bed. "There's no reason
for you to stick around here. I'm sure Alicia's dad will
give you a ride into the nearest town and you can find
some kind of transportation to Flagstaff."

"Do you intend to go to Flagstaff?"

His eyes suddenly veered away from her and he looked out the window as though intently studying the scenery. "I might, later. There's no rush for me. I've got to figure out if we can salvage the plane. That might be quite a project."

She sat down by the bed and placed her hand over his. She could feel him tense. "Hawk, what's wrong?"

He rolled his head slowly on the pillow so that he was facing her. Without expression he said, "You are the one who just told me."

"You know that's not what I'm talking about."

A nerve began to jump in his cheek, and she realized his teeth were tightly clamped. He shrugged.

"I guess I'm having trouble knowing how to thank you for saving my life...then telling you goodbye." His gaze dropped and he studied her hand still lying on top of his.

"Oh, Hawk, is that what this is all about? Can't your macho self-esteem accept a little help from a tenderfoot female?" she teased.

He grinned, and it was close to his natural, humorous expression. "Oh, my macho image might have been knocked around a bit, but I think it's going to survive."

She cocked her head to one side and asked, "Why do we have to say goodbye?" She hoped he couldn't hear her heart pounding in her chest. The answer to that question held all the hopes for their future.

Once more his gaze met hers and the sadness in his eyes caused her throat to tighten in despair. *No!* she protested silently. *Don't say it!*

But he did. "No matter how we got here, and who saved whom, the fact remains that my job is over. I'm sure the insurance will cover all your costs. I'm sorry I didn't get you to Flagstaff."

"But what about us, Hawk?"

He jerked his hand away from under hers. "There is no *us*, Paige. What did you expect? I'm not some tame lapdog that you can come home to each evening. I'm too restless to stay in one place, anyway. But even if I could, I wouldn't want to live on the fringe of your life. I'd want all of you, not just the leftovers when you were through with your work each day."

He was putting into words what Paige had known all along. So why did it hurt so much to know that he recognized the futility of trying to prolong their relationship as much as she did?

Because I wanted to believe in happy ever after and love overcoming all obstacles and that love will find a way. She could feel the tears sliding down her cheeks but refused to try to hide them. "I love you, Hawk."

His impassive expression threatened to completely break her composure. *Damn his stoic Indian heritage!*

"What we shared was very special," he finally said in a low voice. "Nothing can ever change that."

"But I want more than just a week with you, Hawk," she pleaded.

A lopsided smile appeared on his face. "You've always existed in an environment where you got whatever you wanted, Paige, but life isn't always like that for everyone. You and I live in two different worlds. We've always known that."

They both heard the sound of a vehicle on gravel drive up and stop outside the trailer.

"That's probably Alicia's dad. She said he was going to come back to take you into town." His eyes were level and without expression when he added, "You'd better go with him."

She nodded, defeated by his polite, calm attitude. There was nothing for her to say—he'd said it all.

Paige paused at the door to the bedroom and turned. For a moment she thought she saw anguish on his face, but it was gone and he continued to meet her gaze without flinching. "Goodbye, Hawk. Take care of yourself."

"You too."

She was thankful she didn't see anyone as she hastened back to the room she'd shared with Alicia. She gathered up the few things that had survived the past week and walked out to meet John.

Paige felt as though she'd been bouncing in the front seat of the pickup truck for years. Sooner or later she was bound to reach Flagstaff.

John had taken her to a little settlement where she found a pay phone and called the hospital. The news was good. She'd even been able to speak to her father and to explain that she was on her way to see him. He'd sounded fine—much better than she felt, as a matter of fact. *Just remember, Paige old girl, nobody's died of a broken heart.*

John had taken her to his brother's house and explained that his brother was going into Flagstaff that day and could give her a ride. She thankfully accepted their help and began her lonely journey back to her old life. She tried to plan what she would do when she reached Flagstaff—find a motel; go shopping; try to forget Hawk; take a hot, soaking bath; try to forget Hawk; go see her father; eat dinner; try to forget Hawk.

Paige rested her head against the back of the seat and closed her eyes.

Try to forget Hawk. That would be the hardest thing to do. There was so much to remember...

"How would you like to learn how to fish?" Hawk had asked Paige the second day they were together.

"Are you sure fishing is part of the curriculum?" she managed to answer. Her head was still sore and she hadn't felt like doing much.

"Wellll..." He ran his hand through his already rumpled hair. "It's the least strenuous thing I can think of for you to do, under the circumstances." He lightly touched the side of her head.

"Good point. I hope I'm not being graded on my performance as a camping mate. Otherwise, I'd have flunked by now."

Hawk laughed. His eyes were so beautiful—they sparkled when he laughed. She loved to say things to amuse him. "You're in luck. You aren't being graded this week. You've been put on the sick list and relieved of all duties."

She gave an exaggerated sigh of relief. "In that case, let's get on with this serious business of fishing."

By the end of the afternoon, they realized she had a long way to go to get the hang of it. Paige had managed to snag a bush, a limb, two rocks, and made a rat's nest of the line before admitting defeat.

"You're giving up?" Hawk asked with simulated surprise.

"Before you fire me. Yes, I am."

"You mean you don't like to fish?"

"How would I know? I haven't had a hook in the water yet. Is there a chance there *are* fish somewhere besides the water?"

"'Fraid not."

"Then we cannot consider that I have been fishing."

Hawk found some shade by the stream and suggested they rest after their strenuous afternoon. Paige was more than ready to comply. The least bit of exercise and her head tended to swim.

He pulled her head into his lap and softly stroked her hair from her face. "Have you ever been deep-sea fishing?"

"Uh-uh. Can you imagine what I'd do with one of *those* lines?" She relaxed, soothed by his gentle touch.

"Oh, you probably wouldn't have any problem at all. They have everything rigged up for you on the boat so that all you do is cast out, then sit and wait for a strike." He smiled at his memories. "Boy, can that be exciting."

"Do you go often?"

"Whenever the mood strikes me."

"It must be nice to do whatever you want, whenever you want."

"It has its advantages...and its disadvantages. It can get a little lonely."

"Not anymore. Or have you already forgotten you now have a wife that will tag along?"

He'd changed the subject, Paige remembered now, pointing out a bird, then suggesting she go to sleep to rest her head. He'd had several opportunities to tell her the truth, but Paige reluctantly faced that they were during the time when she was still suffering from her concussion.

He hadn't wanted to upset her. Instead he'd allowed her to believe they were married, giving her time to fall in love with him.

The pickup slowed, then turned onto the highway. The relief from the jouncing was tremendous. Paige rubbed her head. She no longer had pain of any kind, but she'd never remembered her lost hours.

From what Hawk told her, she'd only forgotten the call about her father, and the plane ride. If only she hadn't assumed she was married. What had made her assume such a thing?

Because you would never have shared a man's bed without being married, her inner voice pointed out implacably.

Oh, that.

Yes, that.

But I ended up making love to him, anyway, she pointed out.

Only after you recognized how deeply you were in love with him. The need to express that love was stronger than thirty years of inhibitions.

Paige could find no answer to that.

It was dark when they reached Flagstaff. Paige had John's brother drop her off at the mall so that she could find something decent to wear to the hospital. He refused payment for the ride, explaining it hadn't been out of his way.

By the time she found what she needed, it was after nine o'clock. She checked into a small motel near the hospital, called to find out the latest news regarding her father, and decided to wait until morning to visit him. The trip into town had taken more out of her than she'd expected. Paige wondered how long it would take her to recover from her experiences during the past week.

Eight weeks later she was still asking herself the same question.

Her father was more to the point. "What are you trying to do to yourself, Paige, have a coronary by the time you're thirty-five?"

Paige had stopped off to see Phillip Winston at his home. At fifty-four, Phillip looked ten years younger, though his russet-colored hair was freely frosted with silver.

"Dad, please don't fuss. We've been over this before. I am *not*, repeat *not*, working too hard. I am eating enough, I am sleeping enough, there is nothing wrong with me. I'm working the same hours I've always worked." She leaned over and kissed him as he sat in the shade out on his patio. "Besides, I stopped by today to check on *your* health, not to discuss mine."

"You never want to discuss yours," he grumbled.

"That's because there's nothing to discuss."

"If you say so."

"Good. I'm glad to have that out of the way." She settled comfortably in the chaise lounge next to his and sipped from the tall, frosted glass of iced tea that Sarah, Phillip's indomitable housekeeper, had brought out to them. "Your problem, dear doctor, is that you're bored, so you're letting your imagination have a field day."

"I *know* I'm bored, Paige. Why the hell wouldn't I be? I could have been back to work two weeks ago."

"Of course you could have," she agreed smoothly, "and been back in the hospital the week afterward."

"I am not an invalid and I'm tired of being treated like one."

Paige couldn't conceal the amusement in her eyes. "Oh, I don't think Sarah and I treat you like an invalid. I think we treat you more as a child having periodic temper tantrums. That's because that's the way you've been behaving." She enjoyed another swallow of her refreshing beverage while she watched that thrust hit home.

Phillip stared at her, startled. The Paige he was used to wouldn't have been quite so caustic, but he ruefully acknowledged to himself she might have some cause.

"Have I really been that bad?"

"Let me put it this way—I've got patients in the hospital right now who are handling their convalescence with more maturity than you've been showing."

"Temper tantrums, huh?"

"Close."

Phillip sighed. "Okay. I'll behave."

"Oh, we don't expect miracles, love, just a little more effort on your part. Believe it or not, we all want to see you back at the clinic just as badly as you want to be there."

He reached over and patted her hand. "Yes, little mother hen, but please don't patronize me."

Paige's eyes glistened with pain. "Dad, I don't mean to sound patronizing, but you scared all of us with that heart attack. We don't want it recurring."

"Amen to that."

"Look, I've got to run. There's a young patient I want to check on. He went home three days ago, and I promised to visit him."

"Aren't you staying for lunch?"

She glanced at her watch. "Not today. I'll grab something later—and I'll be back to see you tomorrow." She stood up. "Would you like me to bring you a coloring book and some crayons?" He threw a small pillow at her as she opened the sliding-glass door into the house. "That's strange. All my other patients are generally delighted with the suggestion."

With a fond smile, Phillip watched her leave. He was inordinately proud of his daughter and didn't care who knew it. He'd always felt they had a good, close relationship—until recently.

Something was definitely bothering her. Her excuse that she was busy at the clinic made sense, but she'd always stayed busy and had seemed to thrive on the hectic pace. That was no longer true.

He could tell she wasn't sleeping well, and she'd lost weight. Paige had always been slender, burning up calories relentlessly as soon as she consumed them, but now her appetite was practically nonexistent.

Phillip had a strong hunch all of her behavior could be traced back to her week in the wilderness. Whenever he tried to discuss it with her, she changed the subject.

He didn't like to see himself as a nosy parent. In fact, Phillip took pride in the fact that he'd always allowed Paige the freedom to make her own decisions without his influence. So why was he feeling the need to confront her with her recent behavior and demand some answers, like the father of a recalcitrant teenager?

He was worried about her—not only because she was his daughter, but because she was his partner and his friend. Phillip suddenly recognized that had one of his other partners or associates been behaving in a similar manner he would not have hesitated to sit down with them and try to find out what was wrong. That's what friends were for.

The next time Paige came over, he'd approach her as a friend rather than a father to see if he could get her to open up to him.

It was plain that she needed someone, but he had a sneaking hunch it wasn't her father!

The late-August sun continued to beat down on the city of El Paso. Wisps of hair stuck to Paige's forehead and she decided to stop and have lunch somewhere quiet and air-conditioned rather than drive through a fast-food place.

Her young patient was doing nicely and she was glad she'd taken the time to check on him. His corrective surgery was healing satisfactorily, and she was pleased with his progress.

She took the next exit off the freeway and saw a Luby's Cafeteria sign. Just what she needed. With her lack of appetite these days, a delicious array of attractive choices would encourage her to eat.

She remembered the meals she'd shared with Hawk. Hawk. Sooner or later her thoughts always returned to him and to their time together. Paige wondered if he ever thought of her. Oh, how she wished she could quit thinking about him!

It was unfortunate for Paige's peace of mind that she'd no sooner found a small table and begun to eat than Hawk walked into the cafeteria with three other men.

They were all dressed in colorful coveralls, and she realized the cafeteria wasn't too far from the airport. Why had she picked this particular place to eat today?

She watched him hungrily, making a mockery of all of her determined efforts to forget him. The four of them were all laughing and joking with each other and the people behind the counter. It was obvious they were regular customers.

He looked marvelous. *At least you know he hasn't been pining away for you.*

The men took their loaded trays to a table across the large room. She discovered she'd been holding her breath, waiting for him to notice her. He didn't. He sat in profile to her and she had an opportunity to prove or to disprove her theories. For weeks she'd tried to convince herself he had only seemed attractive to her because of the environment they'd shared. Paige had to concede that she found him devastatingly attractive regardless of his environment.

Two women walked by the table occupied by the men and stopped. Paige watched Hawk glance up at them and smile—the warm, sensuous smile that accelerated her pulse rate.

Hastily finishing her glass of iced tea, Paige stood up abruptly. Whatever interest he'd shown in her before, he had none now, and she was making herself needlessly miserable by dwelling on what they had shared.

Ignoring the temptation to go over to him and say hello, she made herself walk out of the cafeteria without a backward glance. They had already said all there was to say to each other.

Hawk glanced toward the door and watched a woman leave the cafeteria. She reminded him of Paige, but that wasn't unusual. Everywhere he went these days, he was reminded of Paige.

He couldn't forget her.

It had taken him several weeks to recover from his injuries, including the ribs. Paige had been right about them. It had taken him several more weeks to get his plane out of that meadow.

He'd also found out why no one had found him and Paige. The control tower had lost track of him in the storm and he was nowhere near where he was supposed to be when they were forced down. They could have stayed there for six months and probably not been spotted.

A tiny curve appeared on his lips at the thought. *That might not have been so bad. Maybe I could have gotten her out of my system in that length of time.*

Who was he kidding? He'd already discovered how difficult it was to forget her. He would welcome a nice case of total amnesia about now. He could remember everything she had said to him, everything they had done together, and at night he dreamed he was making love to her. His memories were driving him out of his mind.

Now he thought he saw her everywhere he went. He shook his head.

"Where've you been, Hawk? I've asked you to hand me the salt three times. You tryin' to save me from sodium poisoning or something?" His friend grinned at him.

"Sorry. I was thinking."

"Yeah, we noticed. Our conversation must be too boring for you, right?"

"You got it."

They finished their meal heckling each other, and once again Hawk tried to put Paige out of his mind.

A few days later he decided that the best thing for him to do would be to look her up—go see her— maybe take her to dinner. No doubt his imagination was building her up too much. If he saw her in her natural environment, he'd be reminded of why they had no future together.

He found her number listed in the telephone book, but when he called he discovered he'd reached her answering service. An answering service. What other woman of his acquaintance had a damned answering service? He refused the offer to have Paige return his call, but he couldn't get her out of his mind.

When Hawk saw the mention in the local paper of a hospital benefit being held he thought about attending. It would give him a chance to see her, maybe speak to her—find out if she was all right. He could treat it as a casual meeting between acquaintances. If he could see her one more time, he was sure he'd be better able to deal with his feelings.

Ten days later he realized how big a fool he'd been. Hawk leaned against the marble pillar of the mammoth hotel convention room, watching the cream of the city's society dancing by, decked out in all their finery. The glittering decorations had turned the room into a magical fairyland. Unfortunately Hawk had never believed in fairy tales. He felt ridiculous in his rented formal wear, unaware of the admiring glances he was receiving from several of the women in the room. Why had he ever thought going there was a good idea?

What if Paige didn't come? Why had he thought she would? Were doctors obligated to attend these affairs?

Hawk slowly straightened as he spotted her at the entrance to the ballroom. Paige wore an ivory gown that flowed around her petite form with flattering attention to her feminine shape. She wore her hair loose around her shoulders, and Hawk suffered a sharp pain as memories assailed him.

Her hand rested lightly on the sleeve of the distinguished man who stood by her side, tall and slim. The resemblance was strong. Paige's father. Hawk felt a slight easing of tension. At least her father was all right—one question answered. He watched them circulate around the room, greeting the dignitaries, making conversation, and the gulf between them had never been more apparent to him.

She was like a fairy-tale princess holding court. Several men stood around her, vying for her attention. Why had she made her life sound so lacking in social contact? She appeared comfortable and at ease, totally in her element.

He'd seen enough. More than enough. He recognized that more than the room separated them. He'd never be comfortable in her environment. He wouldn't want to try.

Paige accepted the lighthearted teasing regarding her appearance with a smile.

"How come you never dress like that when you're at the hospital?" Rob Hartman asked.

She glanced down at her gown. "Because I'd probably trip over my skirt halfway through making rounds."

"No. I mean wear your hair down like that."

Paige knew why she'd worn her hair loose. She'd been thinking of Hawk, remembering how he'd enjoyed running his hands through it. Her father had noticed the new style when he came to pick her up and commented on how attractive she looked.

"Sorry, Rob. It isn't practical to wear it loose during the day." She smiled and absently glanced around the room. A tall, attractive man in superbly tailored clothes strode toward the exit. *He looks like Hawk,* she thought. With a small gasp Paige realized it *was* Hawk—and he was leaving.

"Excuse me for a moment, will you?" she murmured. Without waiting for a response, she hurried across the floor.

Of course it was Hawk. No one else had that indefinable air of authority and arrogance he carried—nor walked with the lithe grace of a jungle cat.

People stopped her repeatedly while she tried to catch up with him. By the time she reached the door he was no longer in sight.

Why had he come? To see her? If so, why hadn't he spoken to her? She could make no sense of his behavior, but long after the evening had been forgotten by others, Paige remembered Hawk's presence at the gala event.

She could think of only one reason why he'd attended—to see her.

Twelve

Paige shook her head at the proffered plate of food. "I can't eat another bite, Dad. I'm stuffed."

Phillip glanced at the plate in front of his daughter. She had only taken a few spoonfuls of food on it, and he shook his head. "Paige, you aren't eating enough to keep a bird alive."

She laughed. "Remember when you used to tease me about eating like a bird—a vulture?"

He grinned. "So you did, as a teenager. But you burned it off before it turned into fat. Now you're burning calories you can't afford to lose." He bit off his next thought, determined to choose a better time to discuss his concerns with her.

Sarah came into the dining room with a pot of coffee and poured them each another cup.

"Sarah, your meal was delicious, as always," Paige told her.

The older woman smiled. "I'm glad you enjoyed it."

Phillip stood up. "Why don't we have our coffee in the den, Paige, so we can stretch out and get comfortable."

Paige had fallen into the habit of spending Friday evenings with her father years ago. Nothing had broken that routine. It gave them a chance to catch up on personal news as well as professional problems they might have. Paige had long since discovered that although they worked in the same clinic, they rarely had time to see each other, except while passing in the hall.

Paige settled back in one of her dad's recliners with a sigh. She couldn't remember when she'd felt so tired. A fleeting image of hiking through rugged mountains flashed before her, but she determinedly shoved it away. That happened in another lifetime—to someone else.

"Paige?"

"Hmm?"

"I'm worried about you."

She glanced up at her father in surprise. He was stretched out in another recliner, looking well and rested. He had been given permission to work in the clinic on a part-time, consulting basis for the next few weeks, cheering him up considerably.

"What do you mean?"

"You've lost weight—you aren't eating—I don't think you're getting enough rest—and it bothers me. I thought you and I were friends."

She stared at him. "We *are* friends."

"But not close enough to share our troubles?"

Puzzled by his serious tone, Paige replied, "Dad, I don't know what you're talking about."

He shrugged. He couldn't force her to talk, not if she didn't want to, but he could read the signs. She needed to talk to someone. Desperately. His eyes were filled with love and concern when he said, "Paige, have you thought about getting professional counseling?"

Was she that bad? she wondered with dismay. Was it so obvious that she was suffering? She'd made every effort to forget Hawk and their time together. She'd managed to put him out of her mind for large blocks of time during the day, but he invariably showed up in her dreams at night until she thought she was losing her mind.

Maybe she was.

She sat up in her chair so that she faced Phillip. Maybe it would help to talk about it.

"Do you remember when you had your heart attack and I flew to Flagstaff...or at least I tried to fly?"

He nodded, unwilling to interrupt now that she seemed to have started.

"Being marooned with another person for a week gives you a chance to know him better than if you'd known him for years." She searched for words to explain what happened between her and Hawk. She wasn't even sure that she herself understood.

"I'm sure it would," Phillip murmured.

"I've never known anyone like Hawk Cameron. He's as different as any alien that might have landed from another planet." She looked up and met his quiet gaze. "I found him fascinating."

She waited for his comment, but he made none. He seemed to be waiting for her to continue.

"Hawk is a loner. He's been on his own since he was fourteen...traveled and worked all over the world...and is content to continue his wanderings. I doubt that he'll ever settle in one place."

Phillip was beginning to understand, more by what Paige wasn't saying than her actual statements. "You fell in love with him," he stated quietly.

Her head jerked up from studying her fingers twisting together in her lap. She stared at him in confusion. "I don't know what I feel anymore. I can't seem to forget him. I can recall every conversation we ever had, everything we ever did together..." Her slight blush gave Phillip enough information to draw his own conclusions. "He taught me so much about how to survive in a wilderness, how to rely on myself and nature's provisions, even though he'd brought enough equipment to keep us in comfort." She shook her head. "I don't understand why I miss him so much."

Her dad smiled. "It certainly sounds like love to me."

"How do you get over it?"

"Why should you want to?"

She shrugged. "I don't have much choice. He made it clear we come from two different worlds."

"You already knew that."

"Yes."

"But it doesn't make any difference to you."

Her eyes slowly filled with tears until Phillip was only a blur. "No. It doesn't."

"So what do you intend to do about it?"

"Not a thing. It takes more than one person loving to make a relationship work."

"Ohhhh," Phillip drew out. "Now I understand. Although you fell in love with him, he showed no interest in you."

Paige could feel the heat in her body at the memory of the amount of interest Hawk had shown toward her. In a low voice that Phillip could scarcely hear, she murmured, "He said he loved me."

"Maybe he does."

"But not enough."

"Now I'm not sure I understand what *you* mean. What sort of measuring stick are you using?"

"He told me he wasn't some sort of tame lapdog to wait around until I had some time to give to him." Her hurt and pain echoed through the words.

It was unfortunate that Phillip laughed. Her eyes widened with pain at the sound.

"Paige, honey, you wouldn't be interested in a tame lapdog that sat around and waited for your attention. Why does that comment upset you?"

She thought about his question for a long while. "I guess because I felt he was criticizing my dedication to my profession. I had already told him I didn't have time for a personal relationship in my life."

"Then I don't blame him for his remark. You had already made it clear you weren't willing to change anything in your life to accommodate a relationship with him."

Surprised at his insight, Paige stared at her father with dismay. "That's right, I did."

"So what did you expect him to do...or say? If he's half the man you've described to me, he would want more than bits and pieces of your life."

"That's true, but that's all I have to give."

"Is it?"

"You're a doctor. You know how demanding a profession it is."

"Yes, and I know that I made some serious mistakes in choosing to let it take over my life."

She'd never heard her father talk that way, and when she saw the pain in his face she realized he had some painful memories of his own.

"I loved your mother more than you could possibly imagine, Paige. She was everything I'd ever wanted in a wife...or a lover. And wonder of wonders, she felt the same way about me. Those kinds of shared feelings are very rare and should be appreciated and treasured. They should never be taken for granted." Phillip paused and swallowed, as though his throat had been constricted.

"In my arrogance I took our love for each other for granted. I was young and ambitious—" he gave a rueful shrug "—and very shortsighted. I assumed we had forever together, but in the meantime I had a practice to build, a living to make, demands on my time to fulfill..."

He faced Paige, the pain in his eyes almost more than she could bear. "Then it was too late to change the habits I'd set up. Too late to arrange my schedule so that I could stay home with your mother." He shook his head. "She never complained, although I knew she felt that she came second in my life. But she was wrong. So wrong. I just assumed that we'd have time together later...always later...at some mystical point in life. I didn't realize that I needed to realign my priorities at the very beginning, because some of us aren't given enough time for all we want to do."

Tears ran down Paige's face as she listened to her father. She had memories of her own that confirmed what he was saying. She remembered her mother's joy when her dad came home early and spent any time with them. Her mother counted the days to his vacation when they were off together, away from the heavy demands of his profession.

Paige had always known how much her mother had loved her dad. She'd never understood until now how much her father had loved her mother.

He had given Paige a great deal to think about.

Paige stared up at the ceiling above her bed late that night, thinking of all she'd learned. Life was full of choices—almost too many. Sometimes one choice wiped out many equally fulfilling ones.

Is that what she'd done by choosing medicine as a career? She'd never cared before. Her dedication was all-encompassing and satisfying. She'd never needed anything more to make her life complete—until now.

She needed Hawk. She needed his calm, level-headed attitude toward life that seemed to keep things in perspective. She needed his love and affection, his teasing, his enjoyment of his surroundings—and his steady warmth in her bed each night.

But how did he feel? He'd made it clear he didn't want to be tied down, hadn't he? He enjoyed his present life-style—free to come and go as he pleased.

What if he didn't want her?

She recalled the day they'd found the river again and saw him once again standing under the hard-driving water pouring over the lip of the falls. She saw the look on his face, the love and desire shining in his eyes when he had turned around and had seen her standing there before him.

She remembered the urgency of his lovemaking, the fierce possession, his loss of control with her. He had wanted her then. Was there any way she could make him want her now? Even if he wanted her, would he be willing to share her life?

A sudden thought struck her. A thought so foreign that she was shaken. Was she willing to share *his* life?

Paige spent many days and sleepless nights facing that thought-provoking question.

The late-September sun beat down on the metal hangar where Hawk was working on the engine of his plane. He could feel the perspiration trickling down his back, underneath his mechanic's coveralls.

He rapped his knuckle against one of the parts deep inside the engine and colored the air with a few pungent statements regarding the engine, the plane and El Paso's hot weather.

Straightening, Hawk rubbed his back, tired from the bent-over position he'd held for so long, and glanced out the hangar door. The blue Texas sky looked like a backdrop to Mount Franklin, sitting there like a crouching cat overlooking the city. He walked over to the water fountain and took a long, reviving drink.

Hawk knew he was in bad shape, but he wasn't sure what the hell to do about it. Not that he hadn't tried— he'd almost killed himself trying.

He still couldn't forget Paige. Seeing her at the formal benefit had convinced him they could never make a relationship work, but it hadn't helped him to forget her. That was the first night Hawk had gone out and deliberately drunk himself into oblivion. Unfortunately it hadn't been the last.

He'd tried to replace her memory with other women. He knew several in El Paso and he began to call them. Only, they seemed different to him somehow. Their conversations were boring. Had he ever bothered sitting around talking with them before? Probably not. He decided he probably wouldn't find anyone like Paige to talk to, but he could certainly replace her in bed.

After the third attempt, he'd quit trying. The damn woman had turned him into a eunuch. Embarrassed, he'd had to explain to his dates that he'd had too much to drink. After he'd left them he'd made damn sure that was the case before he finally went to bed.

Damn her.

Rick walked into the hangar just as Hawk picked up a small wrench.

"Uh, Hawk..." Rick was never sure how to approach Hawk anymore. He was worse than a grizzly with a thorn in its paw. Rick didn't think Hawk would be any too pleased with the news he had for him.

"Yeah?" Hawk was already reaching for the troubled insides of the engine.

"There's somebody here to see you."

Hawk raised his head in surprise. No one ever came out to the airport to see him. "Who is it?" The frown he wore wasn't encouraging.

"Well, I only saw her once, but I think it's the same woman who chartered the plane last summer to go to Flagstaff." He shuffled his feet. "I didn't ask her for her name."

Hawk felt like Rick had just picked up a sledgehammer and swung into his midsection. He could scarcely breathe, and the pain in his chest made him realize his lungs had quit working.

"Paige?" he said faintly.

"Yeah, I think that's her name. Dr. Winston, isn't it?"

"Paige is here?"

Rick nodded, surprised at the stunned expression on Hawk's face. He had no way of knowing that Hawk was certain his mind had finally managed to conjure her up in the flesh since he'd been thinking of her for so long.

"What's she want?" he asked gruffly, staring down at the forgotten tool in his hand.

Rick scratched his head. "Well, she said something about wanting to charter a plane or something...said she only wanted you for the pilot."

What the hell? She needed a plane so she'd looked up her old pal, the half-breed pilot? What kind of game was she playing?

"Tell her I'm busy."

"I did."

"So?"

"So, she said she'd wait."

Once again the air was full of Hawk's invective as he discussed the vagaries of certain women who could take off in the middle of the day and wait around indefinitely to see someone.

Rick waited. "What do you want me to tell her?"

Hawk stared at his friend. He and Rick had met in southeast Asia more years ago than either cared to admit. They knew each other too well for him to try to fool Rick now.

He groaned, knowing he was going to have to see her one more time. "Send her out here."

Rick looked around the large hangar in surprise. "Out here? She'll get dirty around all these greasy parts."

"That's just too damned bad, isn't it? If she wants to see me, she can come out here. I'm not going to get cleaned up to talk to some society dame."

Rick backed away. "Okay, no need to take your bad mood out on me, Hawk. Just back off, will you?"

Hawk stared at his friend in alarm. "I'm sorry, Rick. I didn't mean to come across so strong."

Rick waved his hand. "No problem. The trouble with you is lack of a good love life." He laughed as he walked away.

If only Rick knew just how accurate his teasing comment had been. Hawk didn't need Paige's presence to remind him that he hadn't been with a woman since he'd been with her.

Hawk grabbed a rag and began to wipe the grease off his hands. He stood there, facing the door where she would enter, bracing himself to deal with her one more time. At least he'd make sure this would be the last time.

The door hesitantly opened and Paige peeked around, then walked into the hangar. She wore a sleeveless dress made of some type of sheer material, the skirt swirling around her knees. The style drew attention to her beautifully shaped legs and highlighted her slim ankles. Sandles with high heels accented the delicate arch of her small feet. Hawk felt his body react to her.

Just what he needed—visible evidence that she still had a strong effect on him.

She walked toward him as though unsure of her welcome. As she drew closer he realized she'd lost weight. Her air of fragility was even more enhanced. He stood where he was, forcing her to come to him.

When Paige opened the door to the hangar she was shaking so hard she was certain she'd be unable to walk through it. Then her attention was drawn to the foreign-looking garage area of the charter service. She'd never seen anything like it. The building was huge, sheltering three planes and several engines, all partially broken down.

At first she didn't see Hawk—until he moved. He wore greasy coveralls, bright red, and a grease smear across his cheek. The force of her heartbeat seemed to shake her entire body when she spotted him. He stood there watching her, unsmiling.

Paige had thought about this meeting for weeks. She and her father had discussed the possible outcomes and how she might deal with them. What if he refused her? How could she survive without him? It didn't bear thinking about.

She reminded herself that she'd never been one to sit and wait for something to happen, and she couldn't wait any longer for Hawk. She had to face him once and for all. As she neared where he stood she suddenly wished she'd waited a while longer. She wasn't ready for this!

"Hello, Hawk."

"Why aren't you at the clinic?" were his first words.

"I have Wednesday afternoons off."

"Oh."

He looked down at the rag he held, then continued to clean his hands as though removing the grease from his fingers was the most important thing in his life at the moment.

"How have you been? Are your ribs all right?"

"Fine. I'm just fine. How about you?"

She smiled. How honest dared she be? *I'm misera-*
ble, Hawk. I haven't had a decent night's sleep since I
last slept in your arms. I haven't enjoyed a meal since
the last one we cooked out on an open fire. "Okay, I
guess."

He stared at her, waiting, but when she didn't say
any more he impatiently asked, "What brought you
out here?"

She tensed at his abrupt question. Being close to
him, she caught the slight scent of his after-shave—the
scent that had haunted so many of her dreams. What
she wanted to do was throw herself into his arms, but
he made it obvious she wouldn't be welcomed.

Maybe she should leave. She'd already received her
answer, in his tone, his speech, and his body language. She meant nothing to him.

Or he's hiding his feelings. Remember—he's good
at that. You always had trouble trying to figure out
what he was thinking.

Paige took a deep breath and then slowly exhaled.
"I wanted to charter a plane to go camping...and I
was hoping you'd be willing to pilot me."

Go camping! Was she out of her mind? Hawk's
glance fell, and he noticed her hands. They were sys-
tematically shredding a tissue. A slight smile formed
on his lips, then was quickly gone. *She's nervous. I*
wonder why?

He shook his head. "Sorry, Paige, but I'm not
available to fly you anywhere. Didn't Rick tell you I'm
leaving El Paso?"

Paige couldn't have been more shocked at his words
than if he'd slapped her across her face. In all of her
fantasies the one constant was that Hawk would
somehow be nearby.

"Where are you going?" Her lips were so stiff she could barely move them.

"A Peruvian landowner I met a few years ago called and asked if I'd be interested in coming to work for him. He's got extensive landholdings and decided having a plane and a full-time pilot on hand would make his life much simpler."

"When will you be leaving?"

Her words hung between them, slowly dissipating in the continued silence. Finally he shrugged, then motioned to the plane behind him. "Whenever I can get this thing running again. It hasn't acted right since I cracked up in that meadow in Arizona."

Paige looked closer at the plane behind him. "You mean this is the plane we were in?"

"Yes. It's the only one I have, but I'm thinking of selling it and buying another one before I go to South America. I'm not sure I really trust this one anymore."

He leaned against the wing and patted the side of the plane. It was an affectionate pat, effectively negating his words.

"How did you get it back here?"

"It wasn't easy. I flew a helicopter in and worked on it. Finally had to get some help to get it out of there, but we managed."

"Hawk?" She couldn't hide the trembling in her voice.

His eyes met hers in a calm stare. "Yes?"

"Would you like to come over to my place tonight for dinner?"

His expression never changed. "Why?"

"Because I want to see you again...and talk to you."

"What about?"

She fought to keep from saying *us*, because she knew the answer to that. He refused to accept there was a chance for the two of them. But she was ready to fight for the love they shared. A couple of times since she'd entered the hangar Paige had seen past the stoic facade he wore. He'd missed her. Just as she'd missed him. Somehow she had to convince him to give them a chance, but she needed more time to plan. His intention to leave El Paso threw all of her thoughts out of kilter.

"Do we have to have a reason to spend an evening together?" she finally asked.

"Not really. I just don't see the point myself."

"Please, Hawk. For me."

When she looks at me with those waiflike blue eyes pleading, I'm lost. All of my willpower deserts me. This has to be the dumbest thing I've ever done. I must get some sort of pleasure out of making myself miserable. There's a name for people who enjoy being miserable.

"What time?"

Her smile made him flinch—it was so beautiful. If he hadn't still been holding the grease rag he would probably have dragged her into his arms and kissed her silly, but he managed to restrain himself.

"Why don't you come at seven." She fished around in her purse and found a pad and pencil. She wrote something down and tore off the sheet, handing it to him. "Here's my address." She seemed to be memorizing his features. "I'll let you get back to your plane. I'm sorry to have interrupted you." She backed up from him. "I'll see you tonight at seven." Paige left quickly, before he could change his mind.

Hawk continued to stand there, staring at the door she'd closed behind her. He was going to have dinner with her. He was going to her home to see where and how she lived. In other words, he was going to collect more memories of her to try to forget.

"I've got to be out of my ever-loving mind," he muttered in a gruff voice, turning back to the engine.

Thirteen

Paige hurried to the door when she heard the bell. She didn't care if Hawk knew she was eager to see him. She had rushed home from the airport and industriously planned a menu to dazzle him, then realized what she was doing and laughed. They were so very far past that stage in their relationship. Yet he'd never been in her home. For that matter, she had no idea where he lived, either. None of that was important, she thought as she swung open the front door.

Hawk stood there waiting. He looked wonderful to her, wearing tailored chocolate-brown slacks, a creamy beige shirt that emphasized his dark good looks and a look in his eyes that was the most encouragement Paige had received from him all day!

"Come in," she said with a smile, and stepped back from the door.

Hawk stared at her in confusion. Gone was the doctor image he'd tried to focus on all afternoon. In its place stood a gorgeous woman in a caftan of swirling autumn colors. Bright earrings dangled from her pierced ears, peeking through the riotous curls that surrounded her face and shoulders.

Not fair. Not fair at all, Hawk decided. She ushered him into the living room, where he found more surprises. The place was nothing like what he had pictured. Her home was small, tucked within one of the many subdivisions in El Paso. Her living room looked comfortable and well used—nothing like the picture-perfect place he'd conjured up in his mind. Scatter pillows dotted the room with color and candles scented the air with the subtle smell of spices.

"I'm so glad you came over," Paige said breathlessly. He glanced down at her so close by his side. "I've missed you—very much."

Once again his body betrayed him as it responded to the woman only inches away from him. He turned slowly to her, gently stroking her hair behind her ear. "I've missed you too," he finally admitted to them both.

She slid her arms around his neck, going up on tiptoe to reach him. Hawk needed no more encouragement. His arms snaked around her waist and he pulled her tightly against him. His mouth found hers and his kiss left no doubt that he was hungry for her.

For the first time in months Paige felt as though she had found her rightful place. Her home would always be in Hawk's arms.

Hawk's reaction to Paige made a mockery of all his fine intentions. He'd spent the afternoon steeling himself for the evening, determined not to give away any of his feelings for her. He'd decided to show them both that he could spend one last evening with her and they could part as friends.

As a matter of fact, he was feeling quite friendly toward her. Any friendlier and he would explode! Hawk reluctantly placed his hands at Paige's tiny waist and gently pushed her away from him.

Just as reluctantly Paige dropped her arms from around his neck. It felt so good to be near Hawk once more. She had felt his arousal and was reassured even more that her evening might have a happy ending. He certainly couldn't pretend to be indifferent to her.

"Are you hungry?" she asked, then realized how that sounded. Her face flushed.

Hawk started laughing. He hadn't laughed in months, but the release of his feelings felt great— wonderful. What was the use of denying it? He loved this woman to distraction. He might as well enjoy the little time he had with her.

"As a matter of fact..." he drawled, his eyes dancing.

Paige unconsciously placed her hands on her cheeks to cool them, then discovered what she'd done and dropped them to her side. He rubbed the back of his hand against her cheek. "It's good to see you with some color."

"Yes, well, uh, why don't we go into the dining room?" she asked nervously, and turned away.

The table was beautifully arranged with long tapered candles casting a glow to the room. A delicate bouquet of flowers added color.

"I'll go get the wine," she explained, and disappeared into the kitchen. She took a few minutes to force herself to relax, then found the wine in the refrigerator and returned to the other room. "Would you mind pouring?"

"Not at all." He took the bottle and the corkscrew from her. Paige returned to the kitchen and began to bring out their meal.

By the time they were through eating, both of them were more relaxed. They had quickly fallen into their former easy camaraderie. Paige asked him many questions; she wanted to know everything that had happened to him since she'd left him.

"I'm sure Alicia was upset when you left," she finally offered over the rim of her wineglass.

At least he has the grace to squirm at the reminder, she thought, watching him.

"Alicia was a nice kid. Very helpful."

"I can imagine."

"But she was just a kid. Hell, I'm old enough to be her father!"

"A very precocious father, but I suppose that's true."

"Speaking of fathers, you haven't mentioned how your dad is doing."

Paige sensed a deliberate change of subject. "He's doing great. Chomping at the bit to get back to a full-time routine."

"I suppose you've been pretty busy too."

"Yes, the clinic has been going through some major upheavals."

"How's that?"

"Well, we've hired three more doctors, and I've been cutting back considerably on my hours."

He stared at her in disbelief. "Why would you do that?"

She smiled. "Because that's what I want to do."

A sudden suspicion grabbed him, causing him to tense. "Are you pregnant?"

The look of worry and concern on his face almost decided Paige to put him out of his misery at once, but she couldn't quite resist stringing him along for a moment. "Funny you should ask."

He leaned across the table, studying her intently. "You are, aren't you? You've been sick, haven't you? That's why you're so thin."

"And if I am?" she asked with interest, folding her fingers together and resting her chin lightly on them.

Hawk stood up abruptly and began to pace the room. He'd never given it a thought. Not once. All the women he'd ever known had been experienced and knew how to look after themselves. But Paige hadn't been experienced. He'd recognized that immediately. And he'd done nothing to protect her.

What a bastard you are, he told himself. *In every sense of the word. You were going to go off to another country without even finding out—without even discovering if a child was on the way. Just like your father did.*

Paige stood up and began to clear the table. She'd taken all their dishes to the kitchen before Hawk followed her.

"We're going to get married," he stated firmly as soon as he walked through the kitchen door.

Paige turned around from the sink and stared at him. Never had she seen him so serious. "Why?"

He wasn't prepared for her question. The reason was obvious enough, wasn't it?

"Are you saying that you'd be willing to marry me because I might be pregnant?" she asked.

"Of course."

"But what about our different life-styles, our different worlds?"

A very stubborn expression appeared on his face. "Then we'll have to work something out between us...some sort of compromise. I know I'm not the type of person you'd ever marry, but I'm not going to let a child of mine come into this world not knowing its father."

Paige walked over to where Hawk stood in the middle of the kitchen floor and gently stroked his jaw. "Hawk, you're the only type of person I could ever imagine marrying. I spent almost a week thinking I was married to you, and I've never been happier." She leaned up and kissed him on the cheek. "I willingly accept your most romantic proposal," she whispered.

Fierce joy flooded Hawk at her words. She was going to marry him. He couldn't believe it. They were going to be married! Forgotten were all his plans to spend his life alone. Forgotten were all of his vows not to get involved. Dammit all, he *was* involved! He became involved the first time he made love to Paige.

"When is the baby due?" he asked.

Paige took him by the hand and led him back into the living room. She gently pushed him until he sat down on the sofa, then she draped herself across his lap, her arms curled around his neck.

"Hawk, do you love me?" she asked, staring straight into his eyes.

He'd lost the battle—with himself and with her—but for some reason he felt as though he'd won all the jackpots ever offered. He nuzzled her neck, tasting her, smelling her soft flowerlike scent. "Very much."

"That's good, because when we get married I'm all you'll get...at least for a while."

He raised his head and stared at her, bemused.

"I'm not pregnant, Hawk," she whispered.

"But you said..."

"No, *you* said, and I let you think it." She settled more comfortably into his lap with a little wriggle that created havoc with Hawk's concentration. "You see, I've spent the past several weeks trying to figure out a way to convince you that we could have a fine life together."

He opened his mouth to speak, and she placed her fingertips gently across his lips.

"I discovered that you were the most important thing in my life. More important than my career, even though I enjoy it very much. And I couldn't figure out a way to convince you." She dropped her head to his shoulder so that she no longer had to face him. "I'm ashamed to admit that when I discovered I wasn't pregnant I cried for hours. I had so wanted your baby, Hawk. I was even despicable enough to consider using a pregnancy in the hope you'd be swayed into giving us a chance together."

She kissed him lightly in front of his ear, then followed the strong jawline to his chin, her soft kisses creating chills along his spine.

"I love you, Hawk, and I want to marry you. But I'm not pregnant."

When she glanced up at him she couldn't speak. His eyes glistened with moisture, the tenderness and love in them causing her to catch her breath.

"Paige, love, how can I resist you?"

"I was hoping you couldn't."

He dropped his head on the back of the sofa. "So what now? I suppose I need to call the landowner in

Peru and tell him I'm not coming..." he said, as though thinking aloud.

"Not necessarily. Why don't you call him and ask if he could use a medical doctor anywhere on his staff."

Hawk's head snapped forward. "Are you serious?"

"I've never been more serious in my life. What is that old saying? Whither thou goest?" She smiled softly. "I don't want you to change, Hawk. I fell in love with the man you are. All I want to do is become a part of your life. Is that so hard to understand?"

Hawk couldn't believe what he was hearing. "But you're a doctor. You're already established here. Why would you want to move?"

"That's simple—to be with you. Hawk, I'll always be a doctor. Nothing can change that—it's a basic part of me. But there are sick people everywhere. If you're too restless to stay in one place, fine. We'll both move on."

"I think you've lost your mind."

"No, just my heart."

"I can't let you do it."

"Does that mean you're withdrawing your proposal?"

"No, but—I mean, maybe we need to think about this for a while..."

"That's all I've thought about for months. I have to be honest with you and admit it took me a while to work out all of my priorities. But I have them in order now. That is, if you want me."

"Want you! You've haunted me for months. I tried everything I knew to erase you from my mind." He bitterly recalled some of his more resounding failures. "I just want you to be sure."

"I love you, Hawk."

"Oh, dear God, Paige, I love you too. I just hope we're doing the right thing," he said in a husky voice. He kissed her, and Paige knew it was going to be all right. Love really would find a way.

Her thoughts scattered as Hawk deepened his possession of her mouth, his hands sliding down to the hem of her caftan, then slowly climbing once again. Everything was going to be just fine.

Three years later Paige was still convinced. Everything was just fine.

She turned over in their roomy, double sleeping bag and studied the sleeping man beside her with deep-seated love. She'd discovered a fascinating phenomenon—the longer she was with Hawk the more she loved him. Her love seemed to grow like a prolific plant that had been pampered and fed with the finest nutrients.

She watched him quietly, not wanting to wake him. He looked so tired. He'd been working too hard, which was the reason for their vacation.

Only, this time she'd known what to pack for a couple of weeks in the great outdoors. When they'd arrived back in the States last week, Hawk had borrowed a helicopter from Rick and explained they wanted to go camping—in eastern Arizona.

They'd found a lake fed by underground streams and decided to stay for a few days. During their exploring Hawk had even found them a waterfall.

Peru had been an education Paige wouldn't have wanted to miss. She had grown to love the people in the village near their small home, and fortunately they had come to accept her. She'd been able to teach them how to care for their young ones, and found the experience very satisfying and fulfilling.

Hawk turned over, effectively pinning her into place by throwing an arm and a leg over her. "Move over, you big ox. You don't have to take up all the room," she complained, chuckling.

"Who's a big ox?"

"You are," she muttered.

"Is that any way for you to talk to your dearly beloved?"

"It is when your dearly beloved weighs almost two hundred pounds."

"I see. Does this mean that the honeymoon is over?"

"Of course not. We've only been married three years. Honeymoons are supposed to last up to twenty-five years. After that, we'll be on our own."

He tried to hide his smile, but was unsuccessful. "Are you warm enough?"

"Yes. This new camping gear is great, and so roomy."

Hawk stared up at the ceiling of their tent. It was a six-man tent, large enough so they could move around comfortably. He would never try to do any backpacking with it, but then, he didn't need to.

"Do you want to go fishing?"

She looked at him with suspicion. "I thought you said you weren't going to fish with me anymore when I caught more yesterday than you did."

He smiled innocently. "I changed my mind."

She digested his remark. "Why?"

"Because I love to watch you make all those faces when you bait your hook."

"Oh, Hawk, don't make fun of me."

"But darling, I love to make fun of you, and to love you, and to laugh with you. I love to do everything with you." His actions soon followed the example of his words.

With easy familiarity he touched her in all those places that fanned the flame of her desire, and she was soon lost to everything but him. The years had also taught Paige how to love Hawk, and she delighted in causing him to lose his iron control.

"Oh, honey, you feel so good," he whispered some time later. The only peace Hawk had found in the world was there in her arms. He lay there, trying to catch his breath, while she stroked her fingers through his hair.

"Hawk?"

"Hmm."

"Is it definite we're moving to Alaska after our vacation?"

He lifted his head, then dropped it on her breast once more. "Uh-huh. The letter was waiting for me in El Paso, confirming the date we're due up there. I forgot to show it to you."

"So now we're officially partners. We'll be flying supplies and medical attention to people who are isolated."

"Uh-huh."

"Hawk?"

"Hmm?"

"I have a confession to make."

He raised his head. "You talk too much?" he offered with a straight face.

"That too. But it may have more serious consequences."

He shifted slightly, so that he was lying beside her. "What's wrong?"

"Maybe nothing, but then again..."

"Paige..." he said in a warning voice.

She stared at him uncertainly, then decided to come right out with it. "I forgot to pack my birth-control pills for our vacation." She waited, watching his face apprehensively.

His impassive expression fell into place. *Damn*, Paige thought with vexation. *He can still hide what he's thinking and feeling from me when he wants to!*

"I find it interesting that you've waited almost a week to inform me of that little bit of vital information."

"I know. I'm ashamed. I really am."

"But not enough to have said anything about it before now."

"No, because...well, because I didn't get pregnant the other time we were camping and we didn't take any precautions then either."

He studied her anxious expression for a moment, then grinned. "I take it you're ready to start our family, even if it means in Alaska."

She nodded her head. "Oh, Hawk, it wasn't a conscious decision, but I'll admit that when I discovered I didn't have them, I wasn't sorry."

"You are a sneaky, scheming woman, you know that, don't you?"

She nodded slowly.

"Because if you weren't a sneaky, scheming woman, I would be doing all of this traveling on my own, with no one to keep me warm and keep me company and keep me well taken care of." His tone of voice finally convinced her he was teasing. "So why should I expect the choice of when to become a parent to be left in my hands? Now I know how it feels to be henpecked."

"You henpecked? Hah!" Paige sat up, then discovered her legs were still entwined with Hawk's.

"And I love it," he murmured, rolling over onto his back and pulling her down onto his chest. He pulled her face down to his. "I hope you *are* pregnant," he said in a fierce undertone close to her ear. "In fact, if you aren't, I'm most willing to spend whatever time necessary to see that you do become pregnant as soon as possible."

She sighed, relaxing her head on his chest. "It's that sort of devotion to duty that makes me love you so much," Paige said, closing her eyes with complete contentment.

Silhouette Special Edition

AMERICAN TRIBUTE

AMERICAN TRIBUTE

Where a man's dreams count for more than his parentage...

Look for these upcoming titles under the Special Edition American Tribute banner.

LOVE'S HAUNTING REFRAIN
Ada Steward #289—February 1986
For thirty years a deep dark secret kept them apart—King Stockton made his millions while his wife, Amelia, held everything together. Now could they tell their secret, could they admit their love?

THIS LONG WINTER PAST
Jeanne Stephens #295—March 1986
Detective Cody Wakefield checked out Assistant District Attorney Liann McDowell, but only in his leisure time. For it was the danger of Cody's job that caused Liann to shy away.

Silhouette Special Edition

AMERICAN TRIBUTE

RIGHT BEHIND THE RAIN
Elaine Camp #301—April 1986
The difficulty of coping with her brother's
death brought reporter Raleigh Torrence
to the office of Evan Younger, a police
psychologist. He helped her to deal with
her feelings and emotions, including love.

CHEROKEE FIRE
Gena Dalton #307—May 1986
It was Sabrina Dante's silver spoon that
Cherokee cowboy Jarod Redfeather couldn't
trust. The two lovers came from opposite
worlds, but Jarod's Indian heritage taught
them to overcome their differences.

NOBODY'S FOOL
Renee Roszel #313—June 1986
Everyone bet that Martin Dante and Cara
Torrence would get together. But Martin
wasn't putting any money down, and Cara
was out to prove that she was nobody's fool.

MISTY MORNINGS, MAGIC NIGHTS
Ada Steward #319—July 1986
The last thing Carole Stockton wanted was to
fall in love with another politician, especially
Donnelly Wakefield. But under a blanket of
secrecy, far from the campaign spotlights,
their love became a powerful force.

✑ Silhouette Desire

COMING NEXT MONTH

A MUCH NEEDED HOLIDAY—Joan Hohl
Neither Kate nor Trace had believed in holiday magic until they
were brought together during the Christmas rush and discovered
the joy of the season together.

MOONLIGHT SERENADE—Laurel Evans
A small-town radio jazz program was just Emma's speed—until
New York executive Simon Eliot tried to get her to shift gears and
join him in the fast lane.

HERO AT LARGE—Aimée Martel
Writing about the Air Force Pararescue School was a difficult task,
and with Commandant Bob Logan watching her every move,
Leslie had a hard time keeping her mind on her work.

TEACHER'S PET—Ariel Berk
Cecily was a teacher who felt deeply about the value of an
education. Nick had achieved success using his wits. Despite their
differences could they learn the lesson of love?

HOOK, LINE AND SINKER—Elaine Camp
Roxie had caught herself an interview with expert angler
Sonny Austin by telling him she was a fishing pro. Now she was on
the hook to make good her claim.

LOVE BY PROXY—Diana Palmer
Amelia's debut as a belly dancer was less than auspicious. Rather
than dazzling her surprised audience with her jingling bangles, she
wound up losing her job, her head and her heart.

AVAILABLE NOW:

TANGLED WEB
Lass Small

HAWK'S FLIGHT
Annette Broadrick

TAKEN BY STORM
Laurien Blair

LOOK BEYOND TOMORROW
Sara Chance

A COLDHEARTED MAN
Lucy Gordon

NAUGHTY, BUT NICE
Jo Ann Algermissen